Doctor Bianco and Other

Dla Jonathana —
— z pozdrowieniami
Andrzej Bielawski

Wrocław, 22.10.2021

Maciek Bielawski

**Doctor Bianco
and Other Stories**

Translated by Scotia Gilroy

TERRA LIBRORUM

Terra Librorum
London

First published as *Doktor Bianko i inne opowiadania* by
Wydawnictwo Książkowe Klimaty, Wrocław in 2019
Copyright © Maciek Bielawski, 2019
Translation copyright © Scotia Gilroy, 2021

Edited and proofread by Jamie Lee Searle, Eleanor Updegraff,
Linden Lawson
Cover design by Mimi Wasilewska
Typeset by Mimi Wasilewska

BOOK INSTITUTE

©POLAND

This publication has been supported
by the ©POLAND Translation Program

ISBN 978-1-914987-01-4
ISBN 978-1-914987-03-8 (ebook)

Printed in Poland

'A Mistake' was first published in Panel Magazine (Issue #7).

All rights reserved.

No part of this book may be reproduced, stored in a retrieval system, or transmitted in any form or by any means, electronic, mechanical, photocopying, recording, or otherwise, without the prior written permission of the Publisher.

www.terralibrorum.co.uk

Contents

Translator's Foreword 7

1. Continuation of the State 17

2. Genowefa 27

3. Sunday with Daddy 33

4. The Letter 47

5. Doctor Bianco 55

6. Never Disappoint Anyone 63

7. Little Dogs Bark the Loudest 73

8. A Mistake 77

9. A Space of One's Own 83

10. Little Cards 95

11. Voices 101

12. He Also Once Stayed in a Small Cabin   107

13. The Pit   121

14. The Light of Life   131

15. I'm No Philosopher   139

16. The Crow   149

17. I'll Always Love You   159

18. Wrong Number   165

19. Little Goat   181

Translator's Foreword

Doctor Bianco and Other Stories is the second book by the Polish writer Maciek Bielawski, and the first to be translated into English. His first book, *Twarde parapety* (*Hard Windowsills*), a novel published in Poland in 2016, is an autobiographical account of his childhood in the small city of Świdnica in the 1970s and 1980s. In *Doctor Bianco and Other Stories*, Bielawski becomes chameleonic as he assumes the perspectives of characters from various walks of life, yet the stories are still deeply rooted in a thoroughly Polish reality—in this case, a post-communist one. The book has been critically acclaimed in Poland, and the stories were praised by Nobel Prize winner Olga Tokarczuk as 'brilliant little insights into everyday reality'.

Written in spare, unaffected prose devoid of sentimentality, the nineteen stories in this collection gradually reveal the portraits of various people living in an unspecified Polish town. Many of the stories appear to revolve around one particular residential building in this town and its tenants. We meet an old man who stops buying the coal he needs to heat his apartment so he can afford Christmas presents for his granddaughters, a senile old Holocaust survivor who's suspicious of nearly all her neighbours, two young sisters who become completely fed up with their baby brother, an old woman squabbling with her tailor while a suit is being sewn for her own funeral, a misfit bachelor who helps a neighbour deal with his schizophrenic wife, an art academy graduate (the titular Doctor Bianco) who must face the fact that he has disappointed his parents, and many other intriguing characters.

In the original Polish version of this book, the residential building that these characters inhabit is referred to as a *kamienica*. This word is difficult to translate into English. It's often translated as 'tenement house', but this is problematic because in some parts of the world, a 'tenement house' carries the connotation of poverty and squalor. The word *kamienica* doesn't inherently carry traits of either squalor or luxury; it can be in a wealthy area of town or a poor one, it can be run-down or well-maintained, it can be classy with decorative plasterwork, stained-glass windows and ornate balustrades on the staircase, or more austere and modernist. A *kamienica* is simply a residential building that consists of separate living units—usually constructed in the nineteenth or early twentieth century—in contrast with another Polish word, *blok*, which is used for a taller, more contemporary residential building. As readers of these stories will discover, the people living in this particular apartment building come from different strata of society. While some seem to live hand-to-mouth (such as the alcoholic neighbour in 'A Mistake', the old man struggling to afford coal in 'The Letter' and the man who is desperate to make Christmas special for his family on his low income in 'I'll Always Love You'), there are also people with a more solid footing in life (such as the working professionals in 'A Space of One's Own', 'Little Cards' and 'The Light of Life'). To readers in the English-speaking world who live in cities that are neatly sectioned off into rich and poor neighbourhoods, it might seem odd that people from such diverse backgrounds and with such drastically different incomes would inhabit the same building. But this is a holdover from communist times, when people from various levels of society were forced to live side by side, leading to a levelling out of society that is still a distinct feature of Polish towns and cities even today, and which can cause one *kamienica* to have many diverse tenants.

One of the stories in the collection, 'Never Disappoint Anyone', is told from the point of view of a postman who is so devoted to his job that he develops a special connection to everyone on his route. He has particular affection for the tenants of this building and spends time chatting with them every day. We see the tenants from the postman's perspective in this story, then they appear again in other stories but in completely different ways—seen from their own perspectives in first-person narratives, or from those of the people around them. This book is like a kaleidoscope: the characters reappear from story to story in shifting configurations.

Indeed, 'kaleidoscopic' is the best word to describe Maciek Bielawski's literary style. It's kaleidoscopic not only in the way the perspective shifts and characters come and go, but also in the urgent stream of the stories' narratives, which reflect the quick, impulse-driven thought processes of their protagonists. The narratives jump around between past, present and future, creating a shifting kaleidoscope of the characters' random thoughts. The stories—perhaps more aptly called 'micro-stories'—are condensed and essential, like ephemeral glimpses of peoples' lives that often become a series of loose associations or spontaneous reflections. In terms of technique, Maciek Bielawski isn't interested in solving cases or providing answers. He prefers to position himself as an observer. Like a photographer, he presents snapshots of specific moments without unnecessary commentary. Bielawski once stated in an interview, 'In my stories, I catch the characters at a particular moment in their lives. What happens in the space outside the narrative is not a question for me, but for the reader.'

Within the drab, mundane lives of Bielawski's protagonists, from time to time an element of the uncanny creeps into the seemingly ordered reality, creating an intersection of real and imaginary worlds. In 'Wrong Number', there's a hint of a parallel, incomprehensible reality, and the narrative in 'Sunday with Daddy' splits into two separate levels—the concrete events of the story and a parallel reality unfolding in the protagonist's imagination. In 'Little Goat', the final story of the collection, terrifying explosions and invading soldiers keep encroaching, again and again, upon a typical scene of a father putting his young children to bed at night—an apocalyptic materialisation of dormant fears of war. Although war isn't a lived experience for the younger generations of present-day Poles and the trauma of war doesn't shape their everyday lives as it does for someone like the Holocaust survivor in the story 'Genowefa', Poles of all ages, even the youngest ones, are well aware of their country's war-ravaged history. The story can also be read as a dream-like rumination on parental anxiety.

Some of the common aspects of Polish life depicted in Bielawski's stories might seem exotic to readers in the English-speaking world. Characters pickle cucumbers in the autumn and order coal to heat their homes in the winter. A taxi driver adorns the interior of his car with little pictures of Catholic saints. A character plays an accordion at a New Year's Eve party. There's a brief mention of the Black Volga—an urban legend familiar to all Polish people in which shadowy figures in a Volga, a Soviet-made car popular among the communist elite, cruised around the streets of Warsaw in the 1960s and 1970s, abducting children. In the story 'Voices', we meet an old woman named Stasia who has already chosen and purchased her own grave—a common enough practice in Poland—but Stasia takes it one step further and even orders her funeral outfit in advance of her death. A character in another story mentions that his grandmother always treats meat with respect because 'when a person stood in a queue all day to get some meat, then it was respected.' The oldest geneation in present-day Poland is comprised of people whose habits and worldviews were shaped by war and decades of communism. Bielawski's characters are immersed in a uniquely Polish reality; however, they're presented with such immediacy that their world will feel perfectly natural and relatable even to foreign readers.

Bielawski's stories are also full of references to Polish literature, art and music. In the story 'Doctor Bianco', the protagonist's father hands him a copy of *The Promised Land* by Władyslaw Reymont and asks him, 'What do you think of this book?' This classic of Polish literature is familiar to every Pole, and this scene would be like someone in England mentioning a Dickens or Brontë novel. In the story 'He Also Once Stayed in a Small Cabin', while having a small party on a terrace, the characters enthusiastically quote lines from *Hydrozagadka* (a cult superhero comedy film from 1971)—lines that are recognisable to any Polish reader, but baffling to an English one. In other stories there are references to Polish music, such as 'disco polo' (a type of dance music with simple lyrics that is popular at weddings), and to Polish artists such as the 19th-century symbolist painter Malczewski and the 20th-century surrealist painter and sculptor Beksiński.

Catholicism makes frequent appearances in these stories, bubbling beneath the surface of the narrative just as intensely as it penetrates many aspects of everyday life in Poland. Characters meet with relatives in cemeteries on All Souls' Day. They celebrate Christmas with common Polish traditions such as eating carp on Christmas Eve, drinking *kompot*, breaking *opłatki* wafers together with friends and family, and waiting for the first star to appear in the sky before sitting down for Christmas Eve dinner. The concept of 'apostasy' and the various procedures involved in officially leaving the Roman Catholic Church make several appearances in the collection, and the characters encounter obstacles when trying to defect. In the story 'Wrong Number', a character mentions that his friends who were willing to serve as witnesses at his apostasy started to back out one by one, while the narrator of the story 'Continuation of the State' laments that he's still officially a Catholic because he hasn't been able to find his certificate of baptism, a document required in order to officially leave the Church. While this issue of apostasy might seem strange and foreign to English-language readers, it's a very topical issue in present-day Poland. Leaders of the Catholic Church in Poland have become alarmed at the growing phenomenon of people officially leaving it in recent years. The recent tightening of the abortion ban and the accompanying protests, as well as a decline in trust resulting from cover-ups of child sex abuse by Catholic clergy, are often mentioned as contributing to this trend.

In the midst of the distinctly Polish reality presented in these stories, we see characters struggling with problems and situations common to all of humankind, transcending borders and time zones: loneliness, hopelessness, disappointed ambitions, parental anxieties, daily struggles to make ends meet, the numbing grind of mundane jobs, the longing for deceased loved ones, sibling rivalry, marital conflict and jealousy, battles with addiction, and tensions during family holidays. Most of Bielawski's characters lack something in their lives. Sometimes it's money to rent an elegant summer cabin or buy Christmas gifts. At other times, the struggle is to find time for oneself and one's family, or to pursue one's life ambitions in a world that seems determined to thwart them. The harsh realities faced by Bielawski's protagonists are at times darkly funny and other times gut-wrenchingly sad. Bielawski sets up a magnifying glass on a microcosm of Polish life and allows us to glimpse fascinating, surreal scenes from a tangle of lives whose heartbreak, despair and various anxieties will feel universally familiar. This is where the beauty of translated literature lies—in its capacity to give us glimpses into foreign aspects of our world while simultaneously shedding light on the things that link us in our common humanity.

I would like to thank the editor and proofreader of my translation, Jamie Lee Searle and Eleanor Updegraff, for their excellent suggestions and improvements to the text. I would like to thank Tomasz Zaród of Terra Librorum for having the courage to champion bold literature from Central and Eastern Europe in English translation. And last but not least, my eternal gratitude goes to Michał Marczyk for his careful reading of my translation and insightful feedback, as well as for the love, support and encouragement he gave me throughout the entire period of time when I was working on this book. I couldn't have done it without him.

And now, dear readers, it is my great honour to introduce Maciek Bielawski to the English-speaking world. I hope you will find as much enjoyment in reading these stories as I did in translating them.

Scotia Gilroy

For Małgosia

1.
Continuation of the State

It's like this: you're standing at the checkout, you take three beers out of the basket and place them on the conveyor belt in an even row, and in front of you there's this couple with a kid. They've got groceries on the conveyor belt, they're buying bread, butter, cheese, yoghurt, the kinds of products your wife usually buys, and now, when you think about her, you wonder what she'd say if she saw you with these three beers in an even row. And what she'd say if she saw you looking at that little girl, the child of these people in front of you, while thinking about your own daughters. And how they'd feel if they were standing here with you, with these three beers. What would you talk about? You observe the little girl's father; you watch him pretend to be offended when she refuses to help pack their groceries.

'You don't want to help, so I'll pack them myself and you won't get any yoghurt,' the man says.

You can see tears in her eyes, and you think about how you wouldn't be offended if your daughters didn't help you pack the beers, since you'd rather not have them standing there with you in the first place, unless you added bread, butter, cheese and yoghurt to the basket.

And then you leave the shop and get in your car, and you put the bag of beers on the front seat. No, you'd never drink and drive, you can only drink the beers after you get home, where you'll feel free, you'll put on some music and crank it up louder than usual, louder than when they're with you. You won't have to worry about the volume because the woman who lives downstairs isn't there, and you won't have to think about the one upstairs because bass only goes down, or at least that's how it seems to you. You sit on the sofa with a beer and reach for a book, because you read books, you know that you should read because fewer and fewer people are reading these days, and more and more are writing, so you should support those who are writing, but after a few sentences you don't feel like reading any more, you'd rather get some quick information from your phone, so you flip emotionlessly through some news about doctors, politicians, and other shit that doesn't interest you at all, and you don't even look at the book any more, you don't make any promises to yourself that you'll read it, because you need to be sober to read a book, and you're drinking beer, so the book gets tossed into a corner, and you stare at the screen of your phone and wonder what it is about these short forms that attracts you so intensely even though there's nothing in them worthy of attention.

You recently dreamed of having a record player again, you wanted to return to the time when nobody was listening to vinyl records any more but you still had two cardboard boxes full of them, which someone later abandoned in front of a dorm room. You tell this story every time you chat with someone about vinyl, and you mask your sadness about losing Namysłowski's *Winobranie*, which you bought for two złoty, and Depeche Mode's white singles, which you bought for twenty German marks, behind an easy-going, laid-back attitude, because you *are* easy-going after all, you're a laid-back guy, and even though you're almost forty, mentally you're still thirty, and you want to return to that time because the sound from vinyl is better, deeper, and you already have a record player that your family gave you for your birthday, you have dozens of records, many of which you got from your uncle's collection after he died—a lot of old music, including some of Breakout's best albums. But when you're alone and you can finally listen to them, you don't feel like it any more and just listen over and over again to your tried-and-true CD collection, including the jumble left over from your wedding, all those compilations you made so the band wouldn't play, because you don't like wedding bands, you don't like all that coarse Polishness spilling out of the wedding guests' sweaty shirts, you don't like those fat bellies, even though your own belly is getting bigger and you suck it in whenever you take off your shirt, even though you're alone and nobody can see you, because you still have enough decency towards yourself to hide your size, sitting in an uncomfortable position with a beer in one hand and your phone in the other.

After another beer the music seems too quiet, even though it's already cranked up pretty loud, and if your wife and kids were there, on the other side of the wall, you'd have to turn it down, but instead you're turning it up, and now it's so loud you can't understand the lyrics, the speakers are rattling, and you suspect the music might be reaching the upstairs neighbours now, so you stick your headphones in your ears, close your eyes, and go back to that time, you replay situations in your mind, you think of people you've known, you return to your wedding, and then you change the CD because you need to listen to something more ambitious, something avant-garde, because you grew up on avant-garde stuff after all, really ambitious music, and now Can is coming out of your headphones, but it sounds muddy, it doesn't sound how it did when you first discovered krautrock, and you think maybe it's not the right time for Can, so you switch it for a Niemen compilation you made, which you titled *Next to Us* and gave to your friends, and everyone who got it loved Koterski's film *Porno* and that party scene with the title song, so you listen to a few of the tunes and wonder what's become of you all, the people who used to watch this film, and you switch Niemen off in disgust, jump out of bed, and switch on the radio because you need to hear a voice speaking, you start tidying up the kitchen countertop, you put the butter away so it won't get too soft, then you lie down on the messy bed because you don't feel like making it, and you put on another CD.

You have your idols, you have David Bowie, whose concert you drove to Berlin to see with some friends, and now you tell anyone who'll listen about how they took away your camera at the gate, and how worried you were that you wouldn't get it back and that all the pictures of the old Trabant with East German licence plates were gone for good, but after the concert you went to a room where there were dozens of cameras and a security guard gave back your camera right away and then you and your friends slept in a squat, you cooked cabbage stew to thank everyone for their hospitality and you left a window open all night to get rid of the cabbage smell, and the next day you were reprimanded because heating is expensive. You're happy when your daughter declares that she'd like to buy you a David Bowie T-shirt for your birthday, because he's been such a big part of your life for so many years, and you wonder why you haven't yet made her a compilation of your favourite Bowie songs, even though you thought about it before she was born, you had a list ready, but you never got around to doing it, and now you're letting her listen to random stuff, hits for preschoolers with disco polo beats on the numerous CDs supplied by her grandmother. The only time you play music for your daughters is when you're in the car together. As a conscientious father, you ask them if they like it, and you're happy that your favourite John Lennon song delights them too, but when you glance at them in the mirror, you don't see in their faces the same enthusiasm that appears when they listen to their grandma's disco polo.

Nevertheless, you know that their grandma's a good person, she loves her family, she loves her granddaughters more than life itself and would give them heaven and earth, and because of her saintly goodness you go on the warpath with her over this music, over prayers before meals, over her vision of a loving God and the evil lurking in every corner of the world, you build a front against her so as not to introduce your children into a system which you nonetheless upheld by having them baptised after they were born, even though you have very few ties to the Catholic

Church nowadays and have been saying for years that you're going to leave that system, but you still fall victim to it because you don't have a certificate of your own baptism, so you're waiting for an opportunity to get one, and if it could be done over the Internet you would've been free of the Church's structures a long time ago, and you feel like you're almost completely free, and you express this freedom by not having your daughters attend religion class in school, by not sending your daughters to Communion, because you're not a hypocrite, you don't go to church yourself, so why should you drag your children there? But when you sit down to a family dinner with your in-laws, and your mother-in-law turns to your children and begins to chant, 'Oh sweet Jesus, my beloved one, bless this food, oh my God, my life, bless this drink, too,' you submissively lower your head because you don't want to cause any trouble, and you eat in silence. And you enjoy your dinner.

You're hungry now. There are some homemade dumplings from your mother-in-law in the fridge. You toss them into a pan with perverse joy and fry them until they're a deep, rich brown. Your wife, on the other hand, boils them, because it's supposedly healthier to eat them that way, it's important to take care of one's health, and the foundation of good health is diet: you have to eat healthily, fish shouldn't be fried but roasted in foil, with dill, with some lemon juice, with a bit of butter, with broccoli. No, no, no, you let the oil really sizzle in the pan now, and then you pour sour cream over the dumplings and sprinkle salt on them, a lot of salt, and you pinch off a bit of a stock cube and sprinkle that over them too, to really crank up the flavour, and then you pour some of the hot, brown oil over everything, and it's delicious, so incredibly delicious that you let yourself lick the plate, and then you scoop up the remaining oil from the pan with your finger, and you know it wasn't just good, it was delicious, it was crunchy, it was nourishing, but maybe a bit too heavy given that it's getting late, and now you feel the weight of it in your belly, which you're not sucking in any more because you obviously don't give a damn about your belly since you were just revelling in the pleasure of eating burnt dumplings, and now it feels as if they're oozing out of your pores, and you have no doubt that the momentary pleasure is going to have a decisive impact on you during the night. It's getting late. Beer!

One last beer. It's not too late, actually; it's only ten o'clock. You leave the beer in the fridge and go out to the shop for another one, just in case, you probably won't drink it because you have to work in the morning, but it's better to have it than to feel unsatisfied. You do a quick calculation in front of the cooler in the shop and you end up buying two, so you won't have to come back a third time if it turns out the beer in the fridge and the second one you went out for are insufficient, especially since you've just stuffed yourself with greasy food and might be struck by unexpected thirst. You go back home, reminding yourself for encouragement about your wife's absence, because if she were here, you wouldn't go out for more beers, which you're now drinking not for their taste, but for your need to continue the state you recklessly led yourself into with your earlier purchases, when you stood at the checkout and looked contemptuously at the offended father and his crying daughter, who was going to be punished by not getting any yoghurt.

You have your beers, a safe supply in the fridge, you put some music on, the clock says it's twenty to eleven—late, but early, too—you'll just drink one more beer and then go to bed, maybe you'll even make the bed, so as not to increase the scale of your downfall, so that everything will be neat and tidy, maybe you'll even take a shower, freshen yourself up. You reach for your phone and see a text from your friend who's out on the town; he wrote that the night is still young. You calculate, not for the first time that day, whether it's worth it, and you decide that it is, so you order a taxi and in a few minutes you're downtown at the agreed place, you call your friend but it turns out he's no longer there, he waited for a while but then left, so you head back home feeling glad the meeting didn't work out because it could've dragged on until the small hours of the morning, and you have to get up early and be at work by nine, although you already know that you don't have to because you got an email this afternoon saying you don't have to be there at nine, which gives you a bit of a buffer, thanks to which you find yourself in one shop and then another, and after a while these treks for beer start to scare you. You go home, and without drinking any beer you head to bed, thinking that you'll finally get a good night's sleep because tomorrow you'll be able to sleep in until ten o'clock. You remember to pour the regulation litre of water into yourself; you boiled it earlier, so it's had time to cool down, and even though it's lukewarm, you think maybe it's better like that than ice-cold, because then it wouldn't be good for your throat. You jump out of bed a few minutes past three o'clock and run to the toilet, and while you pee, you feel like you've had enough sleep already, you're quite well-rested, and so you pick up a book even though your head is spinning, and you start reading, you get absorbed by it, page after page, and then after a while you put the book down and start to doze off with the thought that you'll get a good night's sleep at last, because you can sleep until ten o'clock, but the alarm clock rings at seven because you forgot to reset it. Your headphones are still in your ears. You take the CD out of the player. Hits for preschoolers.

2.
Genowefa

There's pounding on our door in the middle of the night. This doesn't bode well. We're afraid to open it. A neighbour once woke us up that way.

'Fire!' she screamed.

There was a fire in the stairwell. A son had tried to kill his parents by igniting a bundle of waste paper in front of the door to their apartment. They collect paper in the neighbourhood; it's a way of earning a few pennies. So, I'm very sensitive to this sound. I listen at the door. Silence. I'm about to ask who's there, when the banging starts again.

'Who's there?'

The pounding gets louder. Then a faint, female voice says, 'Open up!'

It's Genowefa. She's standing there in her nightgown, leaning on a cane. That's how she was pounding so hard on the door—with that cane. The skin hangs loosely on her hands, and a faint outline of her breasts can be seen under her nightgown. There's a wild look in her eyes: they've come again. They're in her room, and she wants me to come down and sort them out. I know these stories; such things often happen in Genowefa's apartment. Usually at night, although another neighbour told me they'd also come once during the day and had taken her engagement ring. No sign of a break-in. According to Genowefa, workers had come into her apartment—the ones who'd been renovating the building and repairing the balconies. My wife suddenly appears next to us and asks me to go down. I need to confront those men. And sort them out.

The lights are on and the bed is unmade. Genowefa stays in the entrance hall while I enter the bedroom. I feel scared, even though I know nobody's there.

'There's nobody here!' I call out.

Suddenly, I freeze: there's a hand on my back. It's Genowefa. She's crept up behind me. Did I check behind the curtain? I check. There's nobody there. She wants me to wait until she falls asleep. I sit in an armchair and look at the old lady—she's so small, barely visible in her bed with the quilt pulled up to her chin. A gloomy room. Two First Communion pictures on the wall. And a little table next to the bed with medication on it, and a telephone with speed-dial buttons. One button has 'grandson' written on it.

You have to watch out for Genowefa: she drops her rubbish bags from the second floor. In the middle of our stairwell there's the 'well'—that's what we call the shaft there. Perhaps they planned to install a lift long ago. Once, one of her rubbish bags burst and there were cooked beets splattered all over the walls and floor.

'Please don't throw your rubbish bags down,' my wife tells her. 'Just leave them in front of your door. Someone will carry them down for you.'

'Are you sure?' Genowefa asks.

'I'm sure,' my wife says, nodding.

I find a note at home. My wife is at Genowefa's and wants me to go down to her. The door is ajar. My wife is clipping Genowefa's toenails. It's difficult for Genowefa; she can't bend down. Genowefa tells us that in Auschwitz, they trimmed their toenails by gnawing at them. I go back upstairs, sick to my stomach.

Genowefa's grandson rarely visits her. He takes her to the doctor and to his daughter's First Communion. He rushes her down the stairs, shouting at her that she's too slow. I often hear it, but I never react. She signed the apartment over to him. He's a tense guy. Once, while passing him on the stairs, I looked him straight in the eyes for a long time, and then followed him with my gaze. I never say 'hello' to him.

My wife wakes me up. Genowefa has come. They're in her apartment again. I need to go and call her grandson. Genowefa asks me to stay until her grandson arrives. She'll lie down in the meantime, and I should make myself some tea. And remember to turn off the gas. She always remembers.

Her grandson doesn't answer his phone. I keep dialling, over and over. He finally picks up—he'll come in half an hour. Genowefa is snoring louder than one might expect from her appearance. I go into her living room because I want to see the apartment. She was the first tenant to move into this building after the war. The neighbours say she doesn't get along well with people. She's suspicious of everyone.

'And she acts like she's above everyone else,' a neighbour once complained to me.

Genowefa's constantly clashing with the woman who lives on the ground floor, whose husband is a hunter. One time, when some Germans came to see her husband's hunting trophies, Genowefa stood in the stairwell and shouted menacingly. It sounded something like '*Schweine, raus!*' The neighbour isn't sure, but she nods her head to confirm it happened like that.

I sit down in the armchair. I've decided not to walk around the apartment; when the grandson comes, he might think I'm snooping, looking for something. Maybe he still remembers the way I glared at him in the stairwell.

I'm woken up by someone nudging me—it's Genowefa's grandson. He looks embarrassed. He's sorry he didn't come earlier, but something came up. I must understand. Does he owe me anything? I ask what time it is. Four-thirty in the morning. Does he owe me anything—that's a good one!

My wife worries about Genowefa. She shouldn't live like that. At her age, you need constant help. And those night terrors—it's from the camp. My wife doesn't like to talk about it; she's afraid of war. She wasn't even able to finish the camp survivors' accounts she was supposed to read in school.

I run into Genowefa on the stairs. She's staring absently into the distance.

'Can I help you with something?' I ask. She doesn't respond.

We stand there for a while in silence. She's gone outside again in her slippers. She can't remember where she lives. I take her hand and lead her to her door. She recognises it.

She asks me to come in, and gives me something for the girls. Chocolate. I don't like taking food from old people. But I take it this time. I'm afraid the chocolate might be stale. My wife checks the expiry date. The girls each get a piece.

And once again, there's pounding in the middle of the night. I open the door confidently, expecting Genowefa. But I immediately take a step backwards, startled. The grandson calms me down. He's going to take his grandmother to his place. But before they leave, she wants to talk to my wife. She wants my wife to come downstairs to her.

We go together. Genowefa asks for her toenails to be cut. One last time. My wife asks if I'd like to try it. The grandson hides his face in his hands, embarrassed.

'No, thank you,' I answer, and then I turn round and pretend to search the apartment for intruders. I re-enact those situations, and tell the grandson that I sometimes come here to check if anyone's hiding behind the curtain. The bits of toenail fly off one by one. Click. Click. Hard little clippings.

3.
Sunday with Daddy

Right before the pedestrian crossing, he always thinks he's not going to make it. As the tram crosses the junction and slowly turns left, the clatter of its wheels and screeching of its steel connectors echo through the neighbourhood. And he stands there, because the light's red. The cars stop. It's about to turn green. He touches his trouser pocket and feels for his phone. With his hand on the phone, he starts running. He should get winded. But he doesn't. He controls his breath. He runs faster. Now he's inside. He validates his ticket. Then he feels a hand on his shoulder.

He doesn't like talking to people on trams. Conversations in taxis, he can tolerate. But those are planned in advance.

'Hello, boss!' An intern has sprung up in front of him. They should have hired him permanently a long time ago. Smart and dedicated, the editor thinks. He glances down at the young man's socks: mismatched.

'I've got such a great idea for an article!' The young man catches his breath, then swallows his saliva. One's throat gets dry and rough in such situations.

Swallowing saliva takes a lot of effort, the editor thinks.

'I've been chasing after you, boss, all the way from the junction, where you crossed on the red light… I really worked up a sweat.'

The editor glances around furtively. Although no one is paying any attention to them, he still feels guilty that he's putting these Sunday travellers, these random people, in his and his intern's company, forcing them to witness this dull performance, this ostentatious exchange of opinions. The office is where such conversations should take place, not a tram. The editor starts to feel embarrassed—not only is he appearing before the rest of the passengers as an editor, but also as a boss. And this word 'boss' makes him feel like a blood-sucker, an exploiter of young workers on zero--hours contracts. Of course, everyone—even this grey-haired man pretending to read a newspaper—knows what kind of principles prevail in editorial offices. The editor himself has written about it a few times.

'My sister…' says the intern, a bit more quietly now. 'Do you remember my sister?'

'The one from the story about the twenty-four-hour shop? What about her?'

'She's got a friend. About thirty, maybe thirty-five. Unmarried—partly by choice, partly because she's shy. Her empty bed is what bothers her the most. She's only got a dog. A mongrel. They're the most faithful—like kids from an orphanage, because they've experienced the worst. They'll do anything to prove themselves worthy… Well, that mongrel croaked.'

'It died,' the editor corrected the boy.

'All right. And may the Lord watch over its soul and its body, buried in the pet cemetery… Did you read about that cemetery?'

'No.'

'That's all right. That knowledge wouldn't help us anyway. So, the dog dies. I don't know why. Let's say it's because of complications from babesiosis. So, she takes the dog and puts it in a shoebox because it's a little dog... Or should I say "was" instead of "is"? No, no—"is". After all, it still physically exists! She puts the shoebox in a plastic bag she got when she bought a PS3 console at Media Markt. By the way, is there a connection between loneliness and game consoles?' The intern's voice trails off.

The editor doesn't even try to think of a response. It seems increasingly clear to him that their conversation has reached the ears of all the other passengers. His eyes meet the gaze of the grey-haired man.

'Never mind,' the intern says, not waiting for an answer. 'The woman packs the shaggy little creature like a parcel and goes to bury him under her parents' cherry tree. She wants to give him a normal dog funeral! Because her parents have a house on the outskirts of the city. So, she takes a suburban bus. She looks out of the window. And instead of seeing the everyday scenes of our city, ruined by billboards and housing developments hastily designed in the 1990s, images of her dog flash before her eyes. She sees him frolicking in a meadow, by a river, in a forest. The images in her mind are real, though some of them, she realises, are rather kitschy. For example, when the dog emerges from the river and shakes water off himself, like in a dog food commercial. In this vision, she watches the drops of water whirl around in slow motion. Or when the dog sleeps with her. Not even at the foot of her bed. She remembers him keeping her warm in the winter. Or when she took Fred to the vet—that was the dog's name, Fred—because he seemed to have inflammation of the anal glands, and he, I mean Fred, peed in her lap. Moments that were both beautiful and cruel. She sees a cross-section of scenes from the dog's life. And her—in that life. It's like running towards that legendary white light when you die. But she's not alone while running. She's participating in a friend's last run. Because that's how it feels. When my canary croaked—sorry, I mean when my canary *died*—I had some dreams. I remember one very clearly. I was flying towards the sun, and when I was so close that I was about to burn up, just like Icarus, I heard my canary tell me in his morning warble: "You turn round, I'll continue on…" So, the woman's on that bus and a number of practical questions pop into her head. Will she find a spade? Will the soil be soft? And would it be appropriate to pray over Fred? It seems to her that she should—because she's a religious woman, after all, so the dog probably was devout in its own way, too, because a dog gets these things from its master, especially when it's a mongrel, and not, for example, a German shepherd, which of course has its own opinions and outlook on life. She's torn from her reverie by a young man who has just sat down opposite her. Her attention is drawn by his square, beautifully sculpted jaw, then by his tanned skin and blond hair. He starts trying to chat her up. He's putting some effort into it, just like on a Saturday night after three chilled shots. But she hasn't drunk three chilled shots, though she wishes she had, since she feels destroyed and terribly lonely because no creature will warm her empty bed any more. But he doesn't notice this and starts talking. He tells her about an architectural design—there are plans to start constructing a large educational and cultural centre in the spring, near the junction where our editorial office is.'

'But it was going to be a residential area.'

'Fuck that!' the intern shouts, then he immediately lowers his voice. 'Sorry. No, it's not going to be a residential area. Everything's planned already, because the polytechnic has connections in the city and is co-financing it. And he, the blond guy, works there as an architect. He's full of great ideas. "Girls will come here all the way from California on roller skates and they won't want to go back, because it's such a beautiful city, this place where my father and grandfather came from... Yeah, I've got German roots, but..." he says, his voice trailing off for a moment, "that doesn't bother you, does it?" "No," says the young woman, because she has found a kindred spirit in him and wants to listen to him talk right to the end of the line, or even one loop longer, although she's already afraid he's about to get off the bus and leave her with the image of Fred in her mind, Fred who's now gone, frolicking in meadows, forests and beds. Faced with this grief, she'll burst into tears. She feels the plastic bag on her lap. Is Fred giving up a last bit of warmth? Why here? the woman wonders. Why couldn't he have done it earlier, when they were alone? Before they'd left home? Why does it have to happen on the bus...?

Thankfully there's the square jaw, a real man of the city, an activist and perhaps a *pro bono* ecologist, because he works at the polytechnic where there's less money and projects are more civically than commercially oriented. Would he be offended if she invited him to the funeral? No, she rebukes herself. She won't do that. He might think she's dangerous. It's not every day you meet a woman carrying a dead dog in a box.

"What have you got in that plastic bag? I see there are some sales on…"

"Yes," she says, flustered—but not by the young man's question. She's flustered because the box is getting warmer, and it even feels like it's starting to burn her legs. The woman lifts the package up a few centimetres. Maybe that's how dogs' bodies react when they go to the other side?

"Bruno." The young man extends his hand. "Bruno Kraft."

"Basia," she says. She feels his right hand in hers; it's the hand of an experienced architect, a man who exists at the very centre of life and who heads out to a building site with all his knowledge instead of just shutting himself up in a warm office, slogging away all day long in front of a monitor armed with AutoCAD.

"Basia Wójcik."

"There's always some kind of sale on," says Bruno, and he looks out of the window as if he were searching for suitable locations for further important architectural projects.

"Yes," Basia agrees, feeling the box getting even hotter in her hands. "That's true."

"People get sucked into this consumerism... I'm not talking about you; I wouldn't know if this is your first or second computer this year," says Bruno, laughing. "But we all definitely buy way too much."

"Definitely," says Basia, almost joyfully. "Definitely too much," she repeats, fiddling with her hair. They stop talking for a moment, the bus pulls up to a stop, and Bruno snatches Basia's plastic bag out of her hands and jumps off the bus. Before Basia manages to scream, the bus pulls away from the stop and only after quite a while does the driver, alerted by other passengers, stop the vehicle. Within half an hour, the police are providing Basia with psychological support. The end.'

The editor laughs. 'Look, I have to get off the tram in a moment. I'm picking up my son; we're going to the theatre today. That story's ridiculous!'

'What do you mean, ridiculous?'

'It's an urban legend... Haven't you heard of urban legends?'

'Of course! The black Volga...'

'That's a classic. And there are many that are far more interesting than that one. You should really check your sources!' He says goodbye to the intern and gets off the tram. He glances at his watch. Not much time. He walks faster. Then he starts running. Once again, he doesn't feel tired at all. The less he runs, the better he can handle running. He's breathing normally. Just like before, at the traffic lights.

He's sure he didn't cross when the light was red.

'Dad, are we going to the theatre?' asks his son. 'Are we going?' He wants to make sure.

'Of course. It starts in half an hour.'

'Yay!' his son exclaims. 'On Friday I told Damian we were going, and he said it wasn't true, so I kick 'em.'

'I *kicked him*,' his father corrects him.

'I kicked him.'

'Why did you kick him?'

'Because he said we're not going. He said people don't go to the theatre on Sunday. But we're going, right?'

They're on a tram. The editor looks around. It's empty—typical for a Sunday. Good conditions for talking freely to his son. They don't often get a chance to talk. A work colleague arranged the tickets for him. He's always at work. Even today! Up close, his son seems slightly taller than before.

'What did you eat at Granny's?'

'Apple cake.'

'That's all?'

'Granny fried pork chops but they burned, and Granddad said they looked like the sole of a shoe…'

The man stands in front of his apartment building, feeling the weight of the box he's holding. He tries to guess what's inside. Too heavy for a computer. He nods to his neighbour from the ground floor who's struggling with her lock again.

'You could spray some WD-40 on it,' he says and heads up the stairs. He opens the door. His apartment is nice and cool. He starts boiling some water for coffee and slices some bread.

'... and Granddad said he'd make dinner himself. He fried some dumplings. They sizzled a lot in the pan because they were frozen.'

'Dumplings or pork chops?'

'I told you already—Granddad didn't eat his pork chop because it was as tough as the sole of a shoe, so he fried some dumplings, and then Mum called and Granddad talked a long time, and Granny grabbed the phone away from him and shouted that the dumplings were burning, and that's why I only ate apple cake. And some potatoes with cabbage.'

The man butters a slice of bread. He bites into it. He looks at the plastic bag. He turns it round on the table. He runs his finger along it. The water's boiling. The man pours it over the coffee to brew it. He measures half a teaspoon of sugar. He puts it in his coffee but doesn't stir it. The sugar needs to adjust to its new environment before it can release its full sweetness.

'Daddy, this is our stop!' shouts the boy, pulling on his father. The editor jumps up and they get off the tram at the last moment. The theatre is right in front of them. They'll make it just in time. Seats twelve and thirteen. Row fifteen.

The doorbell rings. The man walks to the door. He looks through the peephole. The neighbour from the ground floor. He opens the door. They go downstairs. Trouble with the lock again. He goes back for the WD-40. He sprays it a few times into the lock. They wait silently. The neighbour glances anxiously at him. He extends his hand

and wordlessly asks for the key. He sticks it in the lock. It turns. The latch springs back, just like new. He does it a few times.

'That's enough, or it'll jam again!' The neighbour pulls the key out. She enters the apartment. She closes the door. But a moment later she opens it again, just a crack. 'Thank you,' she says.

They have good seats. No one's blocking their view. They couldn't have found better spots. The boy is clearly excited. It's his first time going to the theatre. Although he knows the story of Little Red Riding Hood by heart, he clenches his little fists and stares at the curtain. It smells the same here as it did years ago. Like musty old upholstery. The editor likes that smell.

'I wonder what the wolf will look like.'

'Like an ordinary mongrel,' his father replies absent-mindedly because in his thoughts, he's inside that man's old apartment building. Now the man goes back upstairs and enters his apartment. In the kitchen he touches his cup of coffee. It's the perfect warmth. He takes a sip. He perceives its flavour more intensely than he usually does. The coffee slowly flows down his throat, leaving just the right amount of bitterness on his taste buds.

The man stares at the box. He pulls it towards him.

'Mongrel?' the son asks, surprised.

'What mongrel?' answers the father. Then, realising his slip of the tongue, he says, 'No, sorry, it'll look like a wolf. Just a normal wolf. Grey, the size of a German Shepherd, maybe a bit bigger.'

'It's got to be bigger, because if the granny can fit in it...' remarks the boy.

'Maybe bigger, but not too big...' His voice breaks off and he sees the dog in the box, lifeless and curled up, without its mistress, without the chance of a decent burial. Even worse, when the box is opened, this man's head will appear instead of the branches of a cherry tree. Does the dog deserve such a plot twist? After all, it was just an ordinary, cheerful dog—a mixed-race mutt from an unknown mother and father.

'But bigger than the granny,' says the boy. The editor places his index finger against his lips and whispers, 'Yes.' The lights slowly dim. The curtain rises. There are two puppets on the stage: a mother and her daughter, Little Red Riding Hood.

'Go through the woods, and don't stray from the path, okay?'

'Of course, Mummy!' says Little Red Riding Hood. 'I'll go straight to Granny's house.'

The children react exuberantly to the show. The editor's son watches intently, cuddled up against his dad. The editor can feel that his son's hand is moist. Sweaty. Like the hand of the man holding the cup of coffee while he takes small sips. As the coffee's warmth penetrates the skin of his hand, the skin gets warmer and more slippery, until the cup suddenly slips out of his grasp and shatters on the floor.

'Aha! Got you, Granny!' the wolf shouts. A huge commotion erupts among the kids because the scene is brutal.

A special construction in the form of a mechanical wolf (the result of a collaboration between Polish and Spanish art academies) moves in a way that is simultaneously refined and decisive. The wolf swallows the granny in one gulp, and a thunderous smacking sound comes from the speakers.

'Damn!' curses the man. Then he bends down over the broken cup. He picks up one, two, three shards and carries them to the dustbin. As he's returning with a rag, he steps on some glass. He hadn't noticed that piece; it's hard to see transparent material, and even harder for artists to paint it. This thought strikes him right at the moment when the shard of glass lodges in his foot. A sharper pain than he has ever experienced before shoots through him, even though he has experienced a lot of suffering in his life, mainly physical. For example, at the construction site recently, during archaeological consultations, a hornet stung him. On the neck. Or maybe it was a bee? He thought he was going to suffocate. But the young archaeologist sucked the venom out of him; at least he thinks she did, because he felt something being drained out of his neck. He didn't have time to ask. They'll never meet again. And the pain is so strong now that the man is crouching between the table and the sink, growing weaker. He falls on to the floor, covered in blood. He gropes in his pocket for his mobile phone to call someone or an ambulance. His phone isn't there. Maybe he lost it when he was running with the box.

'Yay!' the editor's son shrieks, and the other kids begin to cheer. 'Granny's saved!'

'She was so deep in the tummy, so deep!' squeals the little girl next to him, but the editor is still in the kitchen where the man is now crawling to the door of the apartment, leaving a red trail behind him on what might be, the editor imagines, his last journey. The piece of glass is sticking out of his foot. The man is already on the threshold between the kitchen and the hallway. One metre from the front door. But he's too weak to reach the handle. And then he hears a key scrape in the lock and there's a long second that feels to him like a minute or even longer, before the handle goes down and stops.

'Come on, just open it,' he mumbles to himself. 'Open it!'

And the door opens. A woman is standing there. She walks up to the man, looks into his eyes and sees terror in them. And a cry for help. She expertly checks his pulse, and when she kneels down, he notices that her knees are slim and smooth.

The woman pulls out her phone. And then the editor sees a flash of white light in front of him, and when the glow dims, he sees a reporter walking away.

'That was great! I want to work in a puppet theatre,' his son says as they get up and head for the exit.

'Anything is possible, you've got your whole life ahead of you,' says the editor cheerfully, although he's still thinking about the woman's knees. 'Do you think I could be a thief?' he suddenly asks his son.

'What would you steal?'

'Money, cars. Anything.'

'Robbing old ladies—no way. But cars… You don't have a driver's licence, though. Why would you want to be a thief?'

'I don't want to. I'm just asking if I could. You know me. You know how I am.'

'Then no. You couldn't. And I wouldn't want you to steal. I'd have to fight Damian again. He makes fun of everyone.'

The next day, the editor is glancing through the newspaper. There's an article on the fourth page. It's titled: 'Sunday with Daddy'. And there's a photo of the editor with his son. Smiling, the editor stares at his own face.

His facial expression looks very absent, he thinks, but he immediately remembers the man and that woman with the slim knees. In the photo, between himself and his son, he sees the woman's legs—from the knees to halfway up the thighs.

He cuts the article out of the newspaper, folds it in half, then folds it again.

He tucks it in a notebook. He could write a short story about it. About a man forced to stay in the hospital for a few long August days. In light of the heatwave that has been forecast, the hottest in twenty years, it doesn't seem like an enviable situation.

4.
The Letter

The letter arrives in September. Zygmunt's daughter reassures him: everything's fine. The word 'fine' looks like it's written in bold. She's inviting him for Christmas. There'll be a place set at the table for him. There has been for many years. His granddaughters are big already; they ask about their granddad. Kasia's nine years old. And Basia? 'Work it out yourself,' she writes, and adds a colon followed by a round bracket.

'Our address hasn't changed. Marcin can't wait to see you, either. He even suggested we take out the tableware set that we haven't used in years. With the little blue flowers, remember? Mum was still alive then. You broke the soup tureen. You didn't want to take it from me; I didn't realise you were washing the dishes. I thrust it at you too abruptly. Wet hands,' his daughter writes. Zygmunt remembers. He was surprised they didn't water down their dish soap. What's the point of all those bubbles?

The letter. He has read it many times. And folded it neatly. In the same envelope. He reads it at breakfast and before going to bed. And after his light supper, late in the evening. He doesn't read it during dinner because he never eats dinner. Breakfast keeps him going till evening. That's how it has been for many years, and it works well for him.

He remembers that day well. His daughter called to tell him not to come. He was watching the evening news. They were talking about coal. There was going to be a price hike on the first of the month. He already knew about that: it was one of those confirmed rumours. He had bought an extra tonne and shovelled it into the cellar himself. He couldn't afford to pay anyone to help. Or to buy presents, for that matter. And then his daughter called and told him not to come because she and Marcin were having problems.

'Don't come,' she said. 'Things aren't good between us.'

He was actually happy to hear this because it wouldn't have been good to show up without any presents. That telephone stopped working long ago. He just has a mobile phone now.

He already knows he won't buy coal this year because of the presents. For Kasia and Basia. To make up for all the Christmases and Saint Nicholas Days. And then some! And for his daughter. And for Marcin, too. He'll put, say, two hundred aside every month. He'll spend three hundred on his granddaughters, and one hundred on his daughter and son-in-law. Why not! Older folks don't get so excited about presents, but they still like getting them. As for kids—it goes without saying. He remembers how Ela used to wait for presents. It was all she could think about. 'Someday we'll have a Christmas without any presents,' he would joke.

He takes out the letter. Things are okay now with Marcin. He found a better job; he'll be making more money. They'll show Zygmunt their photos from Crete. The girls got so tanned! They sat on the beach all day long. The weather was perfect.

Once a week, when he's not on guard duty, Zygmunt goes to the shopping centre. After his first visit, he goes home with a headache. There's so much of everything! A doll? Dozens of dolls! The most expensive is one thousand three hundred. That's more than he earns in a month. Vanessa. It speaks three languages. In the old days, it was so much easier because there was no choice. You took whatever they put on the shelves.

He starts worrying that he won't manage to buy anything. Or that he'll buy the wrong thing. That they won't like it. That he'll finally find something good but it'll sell out. His neighbour collects flyers and catalogues. He complains that he's got a heap of them under his bathtub and he's going to start burning them in his stove. Zygmunt knocks on his neighbour's door. He asks if he can take some of them because it's Christmas, and he needs to find out what's in the shops. He can give them back after Sunday.

'Take them! And keep them!' the neighbour insists.

A huge pile of waste paper. All just from the past month. The flyers and catalogues are full of Christmas adverts, even though it's only November. He could do with a new pot. The old one, with the charred bottom, was bought long ago by his wife. He took *kutia* in it to Christmas dinner. He doesn't even know if they liked it. After the tureen broke, nobody was in the mood for dessert. Or a TV like this one. A flat screen, which collects less dust. Zygmunt sighs and turns the page. The toy section. A doll's house. He'll buy two—for Kasia and Basia. They'll make a neighbourhood.

There's a knock at the door. His neighbour asks about the flyers, whether they came in handy. Zygmunt invites his neighbour in. Beautiful things, and so much choice! If he had a bit more money, he'd buy everything in these flyers for his granddaughters. He won't buy any coal this year, but who cares! He's rarely home anyway. The boss isn't easy on him. He gives him overtime, but is demanding. Availability, that's what counts now! He won't make more than twelve hundred.

'But that's enough,' he adds.

The neighbour sighs. He and his wife have low pensions and barely make ends meet. For Christmas, he'll buy some sweets, maybe a box of chocolates. It's the thought that counts. But after not seeing each other for such a long time… Of course, there's no way around it! Zygmunt needs to hold his head high, not walk around like an old pauper! And give some decent presents. People appreciate that. He would never steal, of course.

Zygmunt goes to the shop. There are no doll's houses. They were in the catalogue, but there's not much merchandise at the moment. They only brought a few doll's houses from the warehouse. Maybe they'll have more next week. There are farms with little horses, and a car repair workshop. 'Shove your farms and car repair workshop up your arse!' Zygmunt thinks. He leaves the shop. He wonders if he should give a coin to the old woman begging at the entrance.

'Please know,' writes his daughter, 'that we've missed you very much all these years. There's always been a place for you at our Christmas dinner table.' Zygmunt doesn't celebrate Christmas. Why would he, just for himself? He doesn't go to midnight Mass on Christmas Eve any more, either, and he used to like it. Those powerful voices, the organ. The joy! But going alone, it's just too sad. Too many memories. It's better just to go to bed early on Christmas Eve.

They're delivering coal. He doesn't buy any; he doesn't even open the door when they ring the buzzer. But his neighbour will buy some if they shovel it into the cellar for him. They won't shovel it into the cellar, so he slams the door. After a while, there's a knock at Zygmunt's door. A small bottle is protruding from his neighbour's waistcoat.

'Just a few drops before the holidays, neighbour,' he says, and then he breaks down and tells Zygmunt that things have got worse with his wife. She started listening to Catholic radio. They don't talk any more. They used to talk. Over coffee, about everything and nothing. About what was happening with his brother: that he got a bargain on an Opel, but that his business was losing money because there were constant problems. His wife was sympathetic. She was capable of sympathy in those days. But now? She says it's his own fault because he lives a godless life. Everything carries the burden of guilt but whoever has God in his heart is freed from it, for a person who acts with God on his side is innocent. They don't drink coffee together any more. They don't talk to each other… The neighbour grows silent, then after a while he leaves.

Zygmunt fills his glass. He closes his eyes. He never used to drink alone. The letter. Ela hadn't wanted to worry him because Mum had just died. So, there were some problems all of a sudden? For no reason? Had things ended between them? Had they stopped talking? Like the neighbour… But now Marcin has found a new job, they went to Crete, they spent all day at the beach. Zygmunt will read about Crete. He reaches for the encyclopaedia. An old edition. No, he won't read it. Everything has changed; let's not be silly.

There's a lot of snow this December, just like in the old days. His shoes leak, so it's hard to walk. Zygmunt ties plastic bags around his feet; he can't catch a cold before Christmas. He doesn't want his granddaughters to catch anything from him. He goes back to the shop. The doll's houses are there! And at a lower price. He'll buy a bottle, too, and invite his neighbour over. They'll break a Christmas wafer together in advance, because on Christmas Eve he'll be with the children. They'll look at the doll's houses. And a hand-painted tie for his son-in-law. Maybe he needs more ties, now that he's earning more money. And a scarf for his daughter. She likes scarves. Like his wife. Daughters inherit their taste in clothes from their mothers. White with black polka dots. 'Polka dots are always in style,' he once overheard on a tram.

He's happy. He can't remember the last time he felt happy. At Ela's wedding? And when he became a grandfather! But that was a long time ago. He can picture his granddaughters' smiles, but he can't remember their faces. Sweet, childish smiles. He shivers. He's cold, but happy. Not even the chill in his house bothers him. He'll drink some tea under a blanket and warm up. He's healthy, even though he's seventy years old. He's never been seriously ill.

It's getting very cold. Minus ten already. There's still a bit of coal left in the cellar. He'll burn some now, then it'll be nice and warm when he gets back after having Christmas Eve dinner with the kids. Hopefully he'll be able to find at least one bucketful of it. It'll last all night. It's nice to get up in the morning when the stove is warm. He doesn't like cellars. Rats run around down there. Rats are afraid of people, but people are even more afraid of rats. Zygmunt would like to have an asbestos suit. He saw one in a film about firefighters. Then they could jump at him and bite him as much as they pleased! He picks up the bucket. You can get cancer from asbestos. There's more coal than he expected. He glimpses some light at the far end of the cellar. And hears faint grunting sounds. He walks in that direction, carrying his bucket of coal. His neighbour is standing on a ladder. He's pushing a colourful box on to the top shelf of a bookcase.

'Good evening, neighbour!' says Zygmunt, setting the bucket down and taking a few steps closer to him. He sees a table top covered with jars and a vice next to it, long unused.

'Speak for yourself,' his neighbour quips, climbing down the ladder. 'Hold this!' He hands him a package wrapped in festive paper and heads up the ladder again. He fiddles with something next to some fruit crates. 'Oh, damn!'

He jumps off the ladder. Behind him a colourful package falls to the floor.

Zygmunt leans down to pick up the package.

'From last Christmas,' the neighbour says, taking the package from Zygmunt and weighing it in his hand. 'A lucky tree. I didn't give it to her. And I won't give it now!' He goes up the ladder with both packages. 'I won't give them to that hag! I won't!'

It's time. Zygmunt's suit, which he hasn't worn in years, limits his movements. His tie is too tight; it pinches his neck. And the presents. Zygmunt forgot to wrap them. He takes off the tie. Much better. He looks again at the presents for his granddaughters. He takes off his jacket and sits down at the table. Two shiny new packages with Zygmunt's rough fingers on them. He gets up, walks over to the stove, and puts a few pieces of coal into it. The flyers and catalogues, now unneeded, are scattered around the kitchen. He'll keep them to use as kindling. He carelessly wipes his hands on his shirt. He goes back to the table. He takes the presents out of their boxes. He assembles the doll's houses in just a few minutes. They're ready! The little dolls are resting in lawn chairs, under parasols, with streaks of coal dust on their faces. The pink umbrellas brighten the yellowed oilcloth on the kitchen table. No instructions, but there are only a few parts to assemble. Too easy for the girls, really… He gazes at the colourful world.

5.
Doctor Bianco

Doctor Bianco is on a bus. A green Autosan. They could've used a newer one, Doctor Bianco thinks. But he likes the worn-out seats and the smell of all the previous journeys. It smells the same as five, ten and fifteen years ago. Because exactly fifteen years have passed since he took the entrance exam to the art academy. Now he's returning home for a celebratory dinner.

Some friends will be there.

'You know them, you know them all. But…' His mother hesitates. 'One guest might be a surprise.'

Doctor Bianco doesn't like those kinds of surprises. He'll feel obliged to talk with everyone. And to be nice, like in the old days. But he feels like being rude and churlish, and dreams of angrily yanking off the tablecloth. Doctor Bianco occasionally has such moments. He wonders if it's okay to feel that way.

It's a short trip from the station. The park terrifies him. They were supposed to install streetlights back when he was in high school. And then he sees the building and the apartment, and a light on in his old room. And someone behind the curtain. Over the bed hangs that portrait from his first year at the art academy. An unsuccessful sketch. He wanted to throw it out, but his mother insisted on keeping it—supposedly it resembled his great-grandfather.

Very soon he'll have to face, once again, the still lifes, the banal landscapes and the series of resized portraits. He'd like to forget about them, but he dreams of them from time to time. It probably happens to everyone. Or could. He rings the doorbell.

His mother gives him a big hug. He forgets about his unsuccessful art projects. He's happy to see his mother; he embraces his father. A burgundy neckerchief. His father has never worn a neckerchief before, Doctor Bianco thinks. But it looks good on him. He peeks into his bedroom.

'You took them down,' he remarks joyfully.

'We've moved them. To the dining room!' His mother takes him by the hand and leads him into the dining room, which is already set up for the celebratory dinner. Wine, cutlery wrapped in napkins, candles.

'Fit for a king!' his father remarks.

'Look!' His mother shows him the portrait in a metal frame. 'It deserved to be framed.'

Doctor Bianco smiles weakly. He takes off his coat. He opens the wardrobe. That familiar smell. But there are fewer jackets in it now. He should take a bath, freshen up. The guests will be here soon. His mother's excited, ready for the party. She reminds herself to take off her apron before it starts.

While his parents carve the turkey, Doctor Bianco walks around the apartment. He peeks into each room. His paintings are hanging on the walls. Things he doesn't even remember. All equally bad. Or in need of improvement. Clumsily executed. In his parents' bedroom, he walks up to a portrait of his mother. How old was she then? Forty? No, perhaps even younger…

'Red or white?' His father interrupts his mental calculations. Doctor Bianco chooses white. They're standing in front of the portrait. His father is holding his wineglass properly. By the stem. He doesn't like fingerprints on the glass. 'These are very good,' he says sadly.

Doctor Bianco runs his finger over the canvas.

They go to the dining room. The portrait of his great-grandfather is above the TV.

'Are you painting anything at the moment?' his father asks.

'I'm making books. I told you already.'

'One *writes* books,' his father laughs, pouring more wine.

The guests start to arrive. The Nowaks are there.

'You look good, and that's what matters in life,' Mr Nowak says to Doctor Bianco, stroking his own enormous belly.

The Kamińskis are there. Doctor Bianco, whom they haven't seen for a long time, is once again complimented on his appearance, and there are also questions about whether he's still painting because they're great admirers of his talent.

'But Malczewski will always be the best,' adds Mrs Kamiński, and then she snatches Doctor Bianco's mother away to the kitchen. They've got things to talk about.

The Kozłowskis arrive.

'Doctor Bianco looks as cheerful as ever!'

Mr Kozłowski currently has some shady business dealings with an art gallery in the Podkarpacie region, and he'd gladly take a few of Doctor Bianco's works. He's already looked at the ones in the cellar. Of course, only if Doctor Bianco is interested. Doctor Bianco isn't interested. But he promises to think it over.

'Painting is a very niche field,' says Mr Kozłowski, 'but one with a future. My cousin buys paintings from students at fine-arts colleges. For just one or two hundred. Bigger ones even for five. It doesn't matter what they look like. But there needs to be a signature on them—a clear signature. These are long-term investments. If some early works by Van Gogh were to show up now, they'd be worth millions. That's what my cousin has in mind. Of course, he means euros.'

Doctor Bianco remembers the surprise. He takes a large sip of wine and looks anxiously at the door. Mrs Kamiński has been to the National Museum in Wrocław. She saw a Malczewski. She loves the perspective in that painting.

'It's alive!' she remarks.

And what has Doctor Bianco been up to?

He makes books now. The guests exchange knowing looks. Doctor Bianco's mother regrets this, though her son has explained to her many times how important it is to him. And that painting is a closed chapter of his life.

The doorbell rings.

Doctor Bianco goes to open the door. Leaving the table is his only way out. By the door there's a print of a horse. It seems to him that the horse has a cat-like gaze.

He changes his mind. He asks his mother to open the door. He goes into the bathroom; he'll wait it out there. He leans against the washing machine. He looks a lot older in the mirror. It's because of the light—very bright, suitable for doing makeup.

'Hello, Anna!' he hears his mother say. He immediately regrets that the bathroom doesn't have a window. He remembers how Anna, her sister and her parents bought themselves ankle-length overcoats. And how they went to church with the price tags still on their sleeves. Doctor Bianco straightens his collar.

'Hi,' he says to Anna, and slowly extends his hand.

Anna gives him a big hug. She hugs him for a very long time and he feels her body against his body and smells her perfume; he'll remember this fragrance forever, as well as the scent of her freshly washed hair and the feel of her cold cheeks, though the autumn is warm this year. He thinks that if Anna jumped up and wrapped her legs around him, it wouldn't change anything.

Because Anna herself never changes, just like Doctor Bianco. Anna's so happy to be there, and Doctor Bianco's glad she is, too, because he likes the smell of her perfume.

It feels good to sit in the company of people you've known for many years, Doctor Bianco thinks after a few glasses of wine. He hardly speaks to Anna, he just watches her talk and marvels at how many conversation topics she has in common with his mother.

'Anna hasn't made a life for herself either,' his mother eventually remarks, and then Doctor Bianco feels bad because he can see that this comment has made Anna sad. His mother apologises and goes to the kitchen to get a bottle of wine. Doctor Bianco remembers the painting he left at Anna's after his second-year exam. They drank a little, though Anna doesn't usually drink, and he forgot to take it. That nude wasn't so bad, Doctor Bianco thinks and reaches for the bottle. His mother hugs Anna and laments that sometimes in the midst of joyful occasions, when everyone's all together, one blurts things out without properly thinking them through.

'And what do you think of this book?' his father says, interrupting the hubbub of the celebratory dinner. He hands Doctor Bianco a copy of *The Promised Land* bound in fake leather with the title printed in gold letters. Doctor Bianco looks at the book and then opens it to a random page in the middle. He starts reading. He becomes immersed in the story. The sound of his father discreetly clearing his throat tears him from his reading. Doctor Bianco gets a hold on himself.

'A good book,' he says.

'Music!' His father jumps up and puts on a CD. Anna Jantar's voice comes out of the speakers and Doctor Bianco's parents begin to dance. The Kamińskis go out on to the balcony to smoke. Doctor Bianco would like a cigarette too, but he doesn't like smoking around his parents. 'You'll ruin your health,' his father used to scold him, even though he himself would smoke from time to time, hiding it from his wife. Doctor Bianco's mother whispers something to Anna, and Mr Kozłowski pulls his wife away to dance. But the Nowaks look glum. Doctor Bianco goes over to them; he feels he should take care of the guests.

'The Kozłowskis,' Mrs Nowak begins, 'are becoming

more unbearable every year. You can't talk about anything with them any more—just art, art, art. People change.'

Doctor Bianco asks about their son, Bartek. They used to play together by the lake.

'He was studying at the polytechnic, he was in his fourth year when he died in the car accident...' says Mrs Nowak, and she sees surprise on Doctor Bianco's face. 'Didn't your mother tell you?'

Doctor Bianco is very sorry to hear this. He remembers the tracksuit bottoms Bartek used to wear, with four stripes down the sides. Did she tell him, or didn't she...? He tries to remember. She must have told him.

Mr Nowak asks his wife to dance. Doctor Bianco goes over to Anna. She looks at him with curiosity, as if he has just returned from a very long journey. Doctor Bianco tells her he feels uncomfortable in this gallery devoted to him, but he understands his parents. And so, what's new in Anna's life? Krzysiek—Doctor Bianco doesn't know Krzysiek—left her. She miscarried twice.

Could he walk her home? She's not feeling very well.

They walk through the park. Anna links arms with Doctor Bianco. They don't speak. Anna wants to walk the rest of the way alone.

Doctor Bianco starts to head home. He glances around for a secluded spot, even though it's late and the park is empty. He vomits behind a flower bed. He enters the apartment. The guests have left. His father's watching TV. His mother's tidying up the kitchen.

'Go to bed,' she tells Doctor Bianco. 'It's late.'

6.
Never Disappoint Anyone

My grandmother fixes her hair and smooths her apron, brushing the dinner crumbs off it. Five złoty for the postman. She reaches for her handbag and takes some coins out of her purse: two, three, three-fifty, four, five.

'Go and exchange these for a five-złoty coin,' she says.

I run to the kiosk to make it in time. Sometimes the wallet is empty; then my grandmother signs for the delivery and leaves any small coins for the postman.

'And if the pension is a round sum?' I ask anxiously.

'It never is,' she says, raising her hand. 'There's always a bit of small change.'

Stefan the postman bows low. 'Kazio came and brought a treat. Good day to you, my sweet!' he says, reciting his monthly rhyme. It makes us all laugh—my grandmother the loudest. As if she were hearing it for the first time. A neighbour says today is the feast day of Our Lady of the Money, and now she'll go shopping and will bring home a bottle to cheer up her old man. But my grandmother doesn't approve of that and rails against her neighbour month after month. This goes on for years, and Stefan grows thinner, more withered. He hunches under the weight of his huge sack. One day, he stands on the threshold with a bouquet of tulips. My grandmother gasps, thrusts out her bosom and grabs her heart, like in a film. Two even rows of false teeth illuminate her face—but only for a moment.

Because it's not a proposal. It's a farewell.

Stefan is retiring. As he hands my grandmother a pile of banknotes, he's giving her some sadness as well. He leaves her in the window, deprived of hope. My grandmother grows thinner, more withered, hunched. And the world accelerates. The TV broadcasts alarming stories about con men, pensioners set up bank accounts. Neighbours make treks to ATMs and enter their PIN codes together. The TV broadcasts alarming stories about thieves. Postmen are reluctant to take money. They relieve themselves of the obligation by presenting false evidence of failed robberies.

'Luckily, I managed to deliver all the pensions before they dragged me into the cellar,' explains one, with a black eye given to him by a friend. He doesn't have to carry money any more. And although my memories of Stefan are fading, although I'm older and the whiskers growing under my nose are getting coarser and harder to shave off with an old razor, I still—and ever more intensely, as time passes—dream of this job. *My name is Benek, short for Benedykt, and I love having contact with people. Please hire me as a postman. In support of my application, I present my belief that there are more letters in the world containing good news than bad. Thank you for considering my request.*

The bearded man lives alone.

'Good morning, Kacper. What's the news today?' he asks on the doorstep, inviting me to chat. About pigeons, for example, because they've covered the windowsill with shit. 'Just to be clear,' he explains, in order to play it safe, 'I don't have anything against pigeons, I like them very much… But they take too long to cook,' he jokes.* And we continue to chat in his kitchen, which hasn't been cleaned since his wife died.

And really, I'm not surprised by this indignation about the windowsill because I like to look out of my own window, too, and tolerance towards birds can only go so far. Right before I leave, he shows me the latest official request for anti-bird spikes. I read it with interest and praise the neat handwriting.

'It's a photocopy. I made it as proof,' he says happily, tucking the letter away in his pocket.

Old people always put off sharing good news until everything else has been said.

I feel at home in this apartment building. If I ever ended up wandering around at night, lost, they would take me in, feed me, and have a kind word to share with me. I wouldn't sing Christmas carols because I'm not religious. Unlike the old woman haunted by her experiences in concentration camps, whose walls are covered with images of saints. I deliver letters to her for her grandson. She watches my every move.

'I hid my rings, but I can't remember where,' she always tells me.

I ask her if she wants me to help. She doesn't.

---

* Translator's note: In Polish, cabbage rolls are called *gołąbki*—'little pigeons'.

'They'll turn up eventually,' she says. 'Or maybe not!' she adds. She starts rummaging for something in her apron pocket.

Then we sit in armchairs in her living room. We usually sit together in silence. She continues to stare at me, tilting her head to the side like a canary, and digs in her pocket again. She pulls out a handkerchief and weakly blows her nose. Nearing one hundred years of age, one doesn't even have the strength to blow one's nose.

'Tell me, Sebastian, is your bag heavy?'

'Very heavy.' I stand up and flex my muscles. 'But it makes no difference to a bodybuilder like me!'

'How much weight can you lift?'

'I can handle one hundred kilos. If I brace myself well and, of course, after a full breakfast.'

'What do you eat for breakfast?' she asks.

'Roast chicken and Belgian fries with light mayonnaise,' I answer, and again we're silent for a while, and she starts to smack her toothless jaws. Maybe she's imagining this unfamiliar kind of breakfast because she still has a great hunger in her mind from Auschwitz. Another time I mention porridge with honey, which I eat every Friday, and a smile appears on her face, but only for a second. Her lips tense up and her face seems even more wrinkled than before.

'I have to go now.'

'You didn't take anything?' she asks as I'm leaving.

On her doorstep, I nod my head in farewell without saying a word.

The stairwell is being renovated. Maybe they'll finally install some anti-bird spikes for the bearded man. I saw the phrase 'anti-bird spikes' mentioned in the local paper. I didn't even think about what it meant until the bearded man explained it to me. You can learn a lot from people.

I usually visit the people on the third floor before Christmas. The younger girl is interested in my bag full of letters. She asks if she can carry it. She walks down the wide corridor and sways from side to side, while the older girl watches from her room with a strand of hair in her mouth. Afterwards, I can give their father his letter.

'We only see each other once a year, Stanisław, but I like your visits very much. They help me get into the holiday spirit,' Bartek laughs, inviting me into the living room. He calls me Stanisław, the old woman calls me Sebastian, and the bearded man calls me Kacper. In fact, all the tenants call me something different—they each have their own special connection to me. I like it that way.

Bartek bought a camera. What an amazing device! With a retractable lens. I wouldn't believe it if I hadn't seen with my own eyes how the giant barrel pops out of a box the size of a packet of cigarettes. We go over to the window. Bartek takes a photo of some guys from the neighbourhood who are sitting under a tree, each with a beer. He shows me a close-up.

'I've been visiting Heniek for so many years, but I've never noticed he has so many pimples!' I remark, surprised at the sight of the bearded man's nose.

'A good lens!' Bartek exclaims with delight.

He recently took some bottles out to the bin. He noticed that deposits had been paid for two of them. He asked the guys under the tree if they wanted them.

'We don't exchange bottles. We just drink!' answered one, and he burst out laughing.

They stayed there for a while, then left. There's nothing to fear in this neighbourhood.

'It's peaceful here unless our team is playing, because then people show up who are already pretty sloshed and it's impossible to sleep,' Bartek says. 'And the worst is when our team loses. Then I wait until morning to take the rubbish out.'

The football fans who live on the ground floor are like that. Two young men and two young women. I'm not afraid to deliver letters to them because we've known each other for years. But they did seriously scare me once. We were standing at the entrance of their apartment, a letter, here you are, thank you, and then one of them suddenly said:

'Franek, who's our goalie now?'

I didn't know how to answer because I don't like football, but I always say that I support our team. When they first heard I was such an avid fan, they wanted to take me to a match. I wriggled my way out of that situation by saying I needed to do something for my mother. They understood this—mothers should always be honoured and respected.

'So, who's the goalie?' he asked, not letting up.

'I have a more important question,' I began. 'Was it a good change?' I asked, raising my forefinger in the air.

And then praise for the new goalkeeper started pouring out, and they claimed he could easily play on the national team, and if he didn't make it within two years, the football fan from the ground floor would cut himself off from the world and wouldn't receive any more letters from me. As for the young women, I can't say anything about them because they just slink around in the background. They're so identical to each other that they look like sisters. Slim blondes in skimpy shorts strolling around, one following the other—that's all I see of them.

But some real sisters—actually from the same parents—live on the top floor. They're both studying Spanish. Oh, what a beautiful language! Sometimes I listen to their songs when I'm not in a hurry. The girls invite me in, and I enter very willingly. Their entire apartment is decorated in shades of red and orange.

'We're crazy about bright colours,' says one of them when I ask where the idea came from. And such intense fragrances! They burn incense.

There's one afternoon I remember very fondly. I was about to finish work, but it turned out that one more letter needed to be delivered. One has to do one's duty, like it or not. As a reward, they treated me to a traditional Spanish dish: *paella*. In the evening, I still had the flavour of it in my mouth. I didn't brush my teeth that night and went to bed with the memory of that delicious dinner still with me. Even I, an old bachelor, can't fathom what they all cook in that apartment building. They fry meat in oil as deep as the oil my grandmother used to cook pork knuckle in. But it's not the same because they fry it fast, while my grandmother always treated meat with respect. Because there wasn't much of it—only on special occasions. When a person stood in a queue all day to get some meat, then it was respected.

One time I tell Krzysiek, the student living on the first floor, 'Have some respect for your heart—you'll get cholesterol from all that oil.'

'But Władek, I like it so much when it drips, flows, sticks! I eat it with my fingers, and the more of it I eat, the more I want. I feel my body growing, it's like a little baby suckling on its mother's breast, feeding on a source of rich nourishment.'

I had no argument against this, since he's such a gourmet. He insisted that I try some. It wasn't bad but the smell lingered in my nostrils all day long, and there's no way to wash one's nostrils, though I really wished that I could.

At the post office, they're surprised that I take so long to do my rounds. But they don't dwell on it, since there haven't been any complaints. I check in at ten o'clock in the morning and finish at eight o'clock in the evening. Halinka, the post office manager, jokes that if I had a woman in my life, she'd straighten me out and I'd be able to take care of everything on my route in a flash. But I like having contact with my clients because a person doesn't only live his own life—a life which, after all, he hasn't really made a success of—he also participates in the lives of others. It's better than television. Everything on television is so abstract, it's hard to relate to it. Only once did something on TV really pull me in; it was a story about a woman who didn't want to have a child, and her mother. The mother conspired with her son-in-law, she approached the matter in various ways, and finally, to help him relax, she started giving him beer. But not too much.

'Because you'll need to stay operational when the time comes,' she advised, smoothing the tablecloth on the kitchen table.

But the daughter dug in her heels and remained steadfast in her resolve. No, absolutely not, end of story.

'Career first, then a child,' she said to her husband when they came home from work, knackered.

And then I fell asleep and dreamed that a child appeared, but it was the girl's mother who gave birth to it. It wasn't hard to guess who the father was. Unfortunately, the mother died soon afterwards, and so the daughter raised the child as if it were her own. With her husband—who didn't admit to anything. At the end of this dream, there was a story in the style of 'one year later': they're walking through the city, she's pushing a pram and taking care of the kid. A proud mum, while her husband walks two steps behind her with his head lowered and his hands in his pockets. It's hard to live like this, with only one real parent between the two. And it hurts him the most when she hugs the child, bathes it, rubs it with soap—their hands are the same, his wife's and her mother's. He remembers them well, and how they smoothed the tablecloth during the decisive conversation.

It was one of those absurd dreams. But as for the film, I didn't like the sneaky plotting and scheming between the mother and her son-in-law. I don't approve of situations like that. Waldek from the fourth floor, for example, lives with his father. He's become unbearable in his old age, ever since he stopped driving his taxi. If he could, he'd live on his son's shoulders so he'd be carried everywhere and could see everything: who sent this letter, and why, what for? It has come to the point that Waldek and I arrange to meet in the cellar so I can deliver his letters to him. First, of course, I send a text message. Waldek's a bachelor too, but only since recently. He had a wife, but she left him. It's difficult to start a new life after that.

'Anyway, it's good to live for a while without anything weighing you down,' he says.

We sit in his cellar and he tells me about dance parties and how the most sophisticated kind of drink is vodka with Pepsi, which his father calls a 'somersault'. He's got a point: you pour some vodka, then you add some Pepsi, and the liquids do a kind of flip. I often imagine it, and Bartek from the third floor promises that one day he'll show me a film on the Internet that's in slow motion, in which you can see how fluids mix together and how shaken Pepsi explodes. He keeps promising to show it to me, but he still hasn't. So I eventually start visualising this moment before falling asleep at night—this shaking and mixing, and then the explosion when the bottle's opened. And now I no longer need to watch it on the Internet. Perhaps I'd just be disappointed, like my grandmother with Stefan.

7.
Little Dogs Bark the Loudest

Mum won't go to the park with Zenek. Mum's friend asked if she could take her to the doctor. She's been waiting for an appointment for three months. The swelling in her leg is getting worse.

Since Mum won't go to the park with Zenek, his sisters will. They love him very much, but with this kind of situation happening for a second time in one week, and it's only Tuesday, the sisters don't love their little brother as much as they did yesterday. Why them again? That stupid Zenek! Granddad was right, though he's dead now: 'Zenek is thick as a brick.'

'How thick is a brick?' asks Hania.

'About this thick.'

'And what's wrong with that?' Hania asks, confused.

'I don't know,' Ola replies. 'Ask Dad.'

Their dad won't be home until evening.

Zenek's ready for the walk—in that idiotic dinosaur hat. Ola will change it as soon as Mum leaves. Since they have no choice but to walk down the street with Zenek, he has to at least look like a normal baby, not a doll.

'It's a Tyrannosaurus rex,' Hania says. 'It looks like a chicken!'

'You don't eat chicken eggs anyway!'

'But you do!' Hania barges in front of her sister so she can push the pram.

Ola's happy to let Hania push. She should be chatting with a friend online right now, but here she is, taking Zenek for a walk. And there's no Internet! Couldn't they just park the pram near a window at home so Zenek could get some fresh air?

'I'm the dad, and you're the mum. And we're going for a walk in the park,' Hania says, starting to play make-believe.

'Don't go off the pavement!' Ola shouts at Hania. 'Push straight ahead!'

Hania adjusts the pram and pushes it straight ahead. She jumps up to see if Zenek's still sleeping. The pram wobbles.

'Stop it!' Ola shrieks. 'You'll wake up Zenek!'

A dog starts to wander between their legs. They'll never have a dog. You have to walk it three times a day.

A hole in the pavement. Zenek wakes up and starts crying. Ola takes a bottle of milk out of a bag and shoves it into Zenek's mouth.

Hania keeps pushing the pram along.

'Slower!' Ola shouts, and she feels so irritated that she's on the verge of kicking Hania. And Zenek too, because she's sick of going on these walks day after day, and what do they even need Zenek for, anyway, this mummy's boy who only causes trouble, everyone focuses all their attention on him while she—she and her sister—are totally overlooked. They're good only for walks. Just walks!

'Our parents don't love us any more,' she says to Hania.

'Yes they do!'

Hania grows sad for a moment. Stupid Zenek! She shakes the pram back and forth. The teat falls out of

Zenek's mouth and milk pours down his cheeks. He starts crying.

'Feed him yourself!' Ola shrieks, shoving the bottle at Hania.

'I can't reach!'

'Then jump!'

Hania stands on her tiptoes. She can barely reach Zenek.

Ola grabs the bottle. Mum's stupid friend! Couldn't she take a taxi?

They walk on in silence.

'... and they actually said they wouldn't go to the park today,' Ola says.

'But they always go to the park,' Hania responds, stopping for a moment.

'... they changed their minds. They're adults,' says Ola.

They turn into a side street. Hania's afraid to go that way, even when Mum is with her.

Fortunately, nothing bad happens. Around the corner, there's the baby box. Their mum showed it to them once.

They stop. There are blankets in the baby box, neatly arranged. Just like in Zenek's cradle.

'A mother who doesn't want her baby can leave it here. It'll be safe.'

'And Mum doesn't want Zenek?' Hania asks.

'... and they decided they didn't want Zenek any more,' Ola continues. 'They have no time for themselves, for their children. They're always stressed out, always in a hurry… Everybody will benefit from it.'

'And Zenek?' Hania feels like she's about to cry.

'Zenek too. He'll be safe.'

'Are you sure?' Hania's hands are covered in sweat, like that time when she put too much paper in the toilet and, after flushing, the water rose almost all the way up to the seat.

Ola lifts Zenek out of the pram.

'I'm sure! Open it!'

Hania can't open it because her hands are too sweaty. She tenses up until her trousers slip down. In front of her eyes, there are pieces of paper slowly floating in the toilet bowl. Once again, her bottom is visible. Ola hates it when that happens because other kids make fun of her. Because of her sister. Always! She walks up to the little window and struggles with the handle herself, with Zenek on her hip.

'… and she thought to herself that she has no use for a husband like that, who can't even open a window,' Ola says.

Zenek starts to moan. Hania looks at Ola's strong hands. Her fingers seem longer than usual because she's letting her nails grow—an older sister's hands. Hania wants to stroke Zenek's head one last time. She reaches out, but the baby's head slides to the side.

'Maybe they didn't want to give Zenek away after all…' Hania's voice trembles.

'… and the dad hesitated, as usual, so the mum had to do everything herself,' Ola says. 'She always had to do everything herself, because the dad lived in his own world!' The handle yields. She puts Zenek inside, but can't close the window.

'Push it shut, so the wind won't make him cold,' Hania pleads.

Ola grapples with the handle again.

A dog starts to bark. It startles them. They run away.

8.
A Mistake

I run into Mr Kuleba in the stairwell. His face is red from vodka.

'Kuleba drinks like a fish,' Aunt Krysia says.

Tracksuit bottoms with padded knees, sagging at the back. Or maybe they're actually long johns, without a fly. Leaning against the handrail, he watches me walk up the stairs. He winks at me, then pulls a quarter-litre bottle of vodka out of his rubber boot and puts his finger to his lips. Our secret. He twists the bottle open, takes a sip, then wipes the mouth of the bottle on his sweatshirt sleeve. He passes it to me.

'No, thank you.'

He takes another sip. I look for my keys.

'My old lady's sick,' says Kuleba. 'An ambulance came.'

I know Mrs Kuleba's chronically ill. But it's not an illness that requires an ambulance. It's an illness that demands constant care. Schizophrenia. That's what Aunt Krysia says. When her husband's in the garden, Mrs Kuleba takes his socks and underpants out of the drawers and hands them out in the street. Men from the Brother Albert charity take them.

The Kulebas robbed Aunt Józefka. One year ago, right after she died, her savings disappeared.

'Euros, złoty. Even dollars, but just a small amount,' says Aunt Krysia, her sister. The Kulebas were the only ones who had a key.

They notified Aunt Krysia a few hours after the ambulance took Aunt Józefka away. Aunt Krysia knows. Two weeks earlier she had borrowed some cash from Aunt Józefka for her friends whose house was only half-built—they still needed to finish the roof. She saw a large amount of money in the credenza then.

I inspect the credenza carefully. I check for secret compartments, or envelopes glued to the shelves.

I feel uncomfortable doing this search. And Mrs Kuleba's going crazy; she keeps trying to climb out of the window. Mr Kuleba shouts in the middle of the night, waking up the neighbours. I run into their apartment. There's a small window in the bathroom—Mrs Kuleba is stuck in it. Her husband is holding her by the thighs.

'Help!' he shouts. 'My old lady's trying to jump!'

I give him a hand. We pull Mrs Kuleba back in. She obediently goes to the bedroom, lies down in their messy bed and falls asleep, as if it were all happening in a dream.

Soon there's a knock at my door. It's Mr Kuleba, holding a bottle. He offers it to me.

'No, thank you.'

He turns away. He stands there, leaning against the handrail. He's crying. I put my arm round him. He's wearing an old sweatshirt that clearly hasn't been washed in years.

'Everything's going to be okay,' I say, even though I know it's not going to be, and that words like these don't mean anything at this point. He's smoking a cigarette. Yellow fingers. Long fingernails.

'What's become of me?' he says. 'What's become of me?!' He stubs out his cigarette in a tin can filled with cigarette butts. He goes back into his apartment. I wait a minute. I want to be sure it's no longer burning.

Another knock at the door. It's Mrs Kuleba, holding a packet of medicine.

'I keep taking them, but they don't work. I've taken five already. Read it for me, please!' She hands me the box. I don't know much about medicine, but I read: suppositories.

'They're suppositories,' I tell her.

Mrs Kuleba squints, trying to concentrate. I nod, and she looks at me as if she's waiting for me to tell her how to use them. Finally, she takes back the packet of medicine and returns to her apartment.

That situation Aunt Krysia told me about—what happened, exactly? I try to recall the details. Aunt Józefka, feeling unwell, knocked on the Kulebas' door in the evening. They'd been neighbours for years. Mr Kuleba led Aunt Józefka back to her bed and told her everything was going to be okay, even though he knew it wouldn't be, and that words like these didn't mean anything at that point.

'The wound on her breast really stunk,' says Aunt Krysia. Cancer. Mr Kuleba put Aunt Józefka to bed. An hour later, he went back to check on her: Aunt Józefka was dead. He consulted with his wife. They searched for money. They decided to wait things out and call an ambulance in the morning. The doctor would determine that the death had occurred a few minutes after midnight.

I go to Kuleba to borrow a twenty for cigarettes.

'Of course!' Mr Kuleba disappears behind the door and is gone for a long time. Eventually, he reappears. He hasn't got a twenty-złoty note. But he's got a fifty. He wants me to take it. I'll pay him back whenever I can. Within this banknote, I visualise not just one, but three packets of cigarettes. Maybe it's from Aunt Józefka's savings?

At the sight of the fifty-złoty note, Basia, the cashier at the corner shop, decides what I need. I receive bread, butter, tomatoes, yellow cheese, cottage cheese (fresh, delivered today), a newspaper (because I didn't get one yesterday), as well as pasta and tomato sauce in a jar, although here Basia hesitates: after all, you can make better sauce from fresh tomatoes.

'Then again, you're a bachelor, so you're not going to make sauce anyway!' she adds.

She also hands me a packet of cigarettes, though with some reluctance. And the change.

She heard that Mrs Kuleba isn't well. She saw an ambulance.

'And Józefka?' I ask. 'Did you see them take Józefka away?'

She disappears into the back room.

Some of Aunt Józefka's furniture needs to be given away. Old credenzas on metal legs. Polished to a high gloss, with impractical glass shelves. Drawers that jam. They smell like Aunt Józefka, as does the rest of the apartment. A year has passed since I moved in. That day, when Aunt Józefka died, Aunt Krysia called and said, 'Józefka is dead. Come visit me this afternoon!'

We're eating cabbage soup when she tells me about the money and the Kulebas. That's also when she suggests I move into Aunt Józefka's apartment. I glance up at Aunt Krysia from my bowl of soup. I recall the smell of Aunt Józefka's apartment; up until now, I've only ever been there to bring her dinner. There's a shred of cabbage on Aunt Krysia's lip. I start to gag.

I give the furniture to Mr Kuleba. We agree that I'll help carry everything to the shed in the garden. Mr Kuleba asks if I could shovel some coal into the cellar. I agree, remembering the cash he recently lent me. I work until evening. Mr Kuleba can't pay me, but then again we didn't discuss payment for the work. He has a proposal: I don't have to pay back the fifty złoty. I agree.

Clearly satisfied, Mr Kuleba says, 'Wait a sec!' He disappears into the shed and returns a moment later, smiling broadly and pushing a green Ukrainian bike. 'Now you can stop taking all those taxis,' he says, and parks the bike in front of me. He's forgotten that I only take taxis on the way back.

In the morning, they're working in the garden. He points out where to dig, and she follows him around with a hoe. The sight of it makes me happy. Finally, a shared activity—something other than the quarter-litre bottle hidden in his rubber boot, the window in the bathroom, and the TV set cranked up too loud. And then she raises the hoe in the air and aims it at her husband. Completely oblivious, Mr Kuleba leans backward. The hoe hits the ground.

Mr Kuleba continues looking around the vegetable patch, and points to other spots that need to be dug up. I move away from the window.

Autumn comes. Mr Kuleba pounds on my door. I open it.

He shouts hysterically, 'My old lady jumped out after the evening news!'

I run into the yard. The neighbours are staring at the body. I go home.

The following morning, there's a knock at my door again. Mr Kuleba's staggering, trying to say something. He can't get a single word out. There's white spittle in the corners of his mouth. His face is flushed from vodka. He waves his hand in resignation and goes back to his apartment.

I watch him through the window. He's working in the garden, pottering around between the vegetable patches. He rakes some leaves.

We pass each other several times a day. When I see Mr Kuleba coming back from the corner shop, I step outside my apartment. I ask him how he's feeling.

'One must live one's life to the fullest!' he says, weighing a carton of milk in the palm of his hand.

It's whole milk. That's what old people drink, according to Aunt Krysia.

9.
A Space of One's Own

The Christmas present that pleases Janek most is the one labelled 'Hobby Box'. He often remarks that having a hobby helps a person stay sane. He says, 'A hobby is a refuge from reality.' If you have a hobby, you have a space of your own! He doesn't like the word 'space', though. He stopped associating it with wild, undeveloped terrain—like a meadow, for example—a long time ago. 'If you have a hobby, you have a world of your own,' he tells his son over and over again. His son doesn't have a hobby; he just turned five. It's good to instil in the child, early in his life, an understanding of the importance of having his own room. Oh! Janek likes that even more. His own room. Janek doesn't have a room of his own. That's why he creates his own space outside the home—at work. In the mornings, the office is practically empty. It's quiet there and you can pursue your hobbies. Janek is interested in cars.

The Hobby Box is a set of cubes made of clear plastic, with little metal balls in each. One ball in the first cube, two in the second, and six in the sixth. The aim is to get the little balls into indentations carved within square tiles that are mounted halfway up inside each cube. Some of the tiles can move, and the sixth tile has a hole through which the balls fall into the second part of the cube. This is the first time Janek has ever seen such an accumulation of challenges.

'Accumulation'—he likes that word. Who came up with this idea? he wonders.

'It must have been quite a malicious person,' Janek says while showing his wife the sixth and most difficult cube. 'Would you like to live with someone who invents toys like these?'

His wife takes the cube from him and tries to get the balls to roll into the indentations. She gives up after a few minutes. It's not for her. There are already so many things to worry about in life that additionally burdening oneself with some Hobby Box is sheer masochism.

'When are you going to repair the dresser drawer?' she snaps at Janek.

After Christmas, everything goes back to normal. No more sleeping till noon, no more walks in the park, no more leftovers. Janek feels great. He doesn't understand his colleagues—after Christmas they complain about going back to work. They grumble that Christmas Eve fell on a Saturday this year, which meant it wasn't a long weekend. Janek likes going back to work. Some peace at last. He'll browse through the automotive news. Mercedes is about to start installing headlights that illuminate bends in the road. Janek imagines driving on winding roads and seeing perfectly illuminated bends. It moves him to think of the engineers who designed these headlights. So simple, but so brilliant. Like airbags or headrests. He wipes away a tear.

Seven in the morning. They're ready to leave. Janek adjusts his son's hat because the winter's harsh this year. He goes back to the bedroom to get his phone. He glances at the Hobby Box. He pulls out the first cube and gets the little ball into the indentation in just a few seconds. Excellent! he thinks. I'm in good form after Christmas! Before Christmas, he promised himself he wouldn't pig out. He doesn't like the phrase 'pig out'. He puts the cube back in the box. He takes it out again. And once again, he aims perfectly and gets the ball in the indentation. And so as not to stop at an even score, he gets it in a third time.

The engine starts on the first try. They really knew how to make cars in the old days, Janek thinks. It's a twenty--year-old Volkswagen. Apparently, you can install such curve-adaptive headlights even in an old Volkswagen Golf. For Janek, this is the third essential feature in a car—after headrests and airbags. Actually, it's the fourth, he corrects himself, because seat belts are the most important. He imagines a head-on collision. The driver of an approaching car loses control of the steering wheel and drifts into Janek's lane, hitting the corner of the Volkswagen. The airbag inflates, there's a hiss like the sound in city buses just before the door closes, and Janek's head lands on the soft airbag, then bounces back and stops on the headrest. Sometimes, when Janek's in a lousy mood, for example when there are more people than usual at work in the morning and Janek can't concentrate on his automotive hobby, he imagines that the airbag doesn't inflate, but he never takes it to the moment when his head is about to hit the steering wheel. Volkswagen Golfs have hard steering wheels. For a while now Janek's been promising himself that he'll buy a soft cover for his, but something always gets in the way… Once when he was heading out to buy one, his son suddenly came down with a fever, so Janek had to stay home with him because his wife was attending a flower-arranging class. The class cost a fortune, so there was no way she could miss it. It would have been great if they'd given him that kind of steering wheel cover for Christmas. It doesn't matter what colour, as long as it's not yellow. He doesn't want his car to look like an Easter egg. If he had a soft cover on his steering wheel, he wonders if he could imagine, right to the end, a head-on collision with an uninflated airbag.

There's nobody in the office. Mercedes isn't going to include curve-adaptive headlights in its entry-level packages. Janek squirms in his chair and glances furtively around the room. Bartek's got his headphones on. Apparently he listens to recovery testimonials. People say his wife is a recovering shopaholic. Bartek has been suffering; he opened a new bank account. Janek reaches into his jacket pocket for a cube. He takes out the second one. He turns round; he doesn't want anyone to see, even though hardly anyone is there. He fiddles with the cube. Three seconds and the first ball rolls into the cavity. The second ball slides down the walls. He's almost got it in when he suddenly hears footsteps.

'Merry belated Christmas!' says Bartek, then he walks away.

The first ball rolls out of the indentation. Another attempt. The first ball rolls into the indentation. The second ball slides down the walls of the cube. Janek sees a car's headlights in his lane and when the second ball is a millimetre away from its destination, he starts to wonder which version of the accident to apply—with or without the airbag. He decides on the version with the airbag, since he still doesn't have that damn steering wheel cover! He can buy one today, maybe he'll manage—after all, it's Tuesday and Jola doesn't have her flower-arranging class. Janek will go to the shop and buy one. But definitely not the fake-fur one because holding it would feel strange. He'll get one made of foam because it supposedly absorbs sweat well, which means his hands won't slip off the steering wheel when he turns sharply. The airbag expands, there's a hiss like the sound on a bus before the door closes, his head lands safely on the headrest. The second ball lands in the indentation. Janek repeats the puzzle. It takes him just a few seconds to get both balls in the indentations.

Janek loves his wife, so he never puts her in the passenger seat during these simulations. Nor his son; he's too young to die. The whole family chipped in to buy a child seat. His brother-in-law's son was impressed. The poor boy has been riding in his family car for years without a child seat; he's only got a booster seat. His brother-in-law isn't even convinced by a YouTube video showing what happens to a child who's sitting on something like that during a collision. His brother-in-law only cares about saving his own arse. He's buying another car—it's only five years old, and he's buying it directly from the original German owner. It's incomprehensible to Janek how someone can be that selfish. How can someone not love their own child? Unless those stories about Kasia aren't just rumours. People compensate in various ways for their failures in life.

Jola's sitting at the kitchen table. She's working on the first cube. Janek puts down the second cube and picks up the third. It's been a long time since they've been so quiet with one another. They're concentrating on the cubes. It's strange not speaking. Usually, it's 'How was work, how was preschool?' But now they're not saying anything, just sitting there with the cubes. Whoever invented this Hobby Box must be an unbearable person, thinks Janek, and when he sees the car's headlights in his lane, he hears his wife shriek: 'Got it!'

The last time she shrieked like that was on the shooting range fifteen years ago, when she won a rose for Janek. It was a bit embarrassing; thankfully none of his friends saw her presenting him with that paper flower. Janek looks up, smiles at his wife, then continues to struggle with the third cube. The first ball, the second ball...

'How was it at work, after Christmas?' Jola asks.

'Just a sec,' says Janek, although he doesn't like that expression, and he keeps grappling with the cube.

Jola runs over to their son. He must have bumped into something because he's shrieking like the siren on a fire engine—that's what Janek's mother-in-law says. Every time the kid cries, Janek's mother-in-law mentions the fire engine. But nothing's on fire, thinks Janek with irritation, and he slowly goes over to see what happened. After all, what can possibly happen in a room that has been specially arranged so the child can't get hurt? There are plastic caps on the corners of the furniture and the windows are secured with hooks. That probably wasn't the best idea, actually, because now Janek has to unhook them whenever they need to air out the room. His wife's too short to reach the hooks. 'She queued up to get some common sense,' Janek often jokes. *But they ran out before she could get any!* he adds in his mind, because after the last time he told that joke they didn't speak to each other for a whole week, which was a record in the history of their fifteen-year marriage, the tenth anniversary of which was marked by the birth of their son, Kuba. When Kuba came into the world, he got his own room. His own space. Janek doesn't like that word.

Janek gets up at six. He makes coffee, brushes his teeth, shaves, and makes some sandwiches. He reaches for the Hobby Box. The first cube—under five seconds. The second one—under ten. The third one—a dangerous four minutes. He repeats it. Five, three, two. One more time. Four, three, two. He resumes his morning tasks. He adjusts Kuba's hat because it's a harsh winter this year. The Volkswagen starts on the first try. In the reflection in the shop window opposite, Janek sees only one headlight. The bulb is dead! In the type of headlights that follow the road, the bulbs signal in advance that they're about to burn out. This means you can do something about it. Buy some at a petrol station. Replace them. Not put yourself and other drivers at the risk of a fender-bender. Janek takes out the first cube. Three seconds. The second cube—five. The third—one minute! The engine's warmed up. They drive off.

One headlight appears in Janek's lane, the version with the airbag expanding, the hiss like on a bus before the door closes, his head on the headrest.

Light traffic; it's the first week after Christmas. A long weekend—you can take one if you want, but it's easier to enjoy it if you don't have kids. Janek thinks about the engineers who came up with the idea of driving with headlights on during the day. It makes the car more visible, and in shade you wouldn't see it at all without headlights. This thought moves him. So simple, yet so brilliant. Once again, he won't be buying a steering wheel cover, because he'll need to buy a new headlight bulb and change it. Two hours of his day! Those conmen will want the bulb to be replaced there, at the car repair workshop. This is all I'll give them! And in his mind he gives them a *bras d'honneur*.

The next day, the office is already full by nine o'clock. The smell of coffee being brewed. He won't browse through the automotive news. Bartek is sitting at his desk without headphones on. He's talking on the phone.

'You're going to ruin us!' he shouts.

The office falls silent. Bartek rises from his desk. Janek takes out the fourth cube. He gets the balls into the indentations in less than a minute. After that—the first, second and third ones. Bartek comes up to him, he's about to say something, but he just waves his hand and goes back to his desk. Jola calls—Janek needs to come home straight after work because the hours of the flower-arranging class have changed in the new year. Janek says goodbye to his wife in a cold tone of voice, but then he immediately texts her a heart. He'll get the bulb for his headlight tomorrow. He finishes the first, second and third cube. During the fourth, he's interrupted by a phone call. And it continues like that all day long, until four o'clock. The other bulb is burned out too. While the engine warms up, he arranges the balls in the fourth, third, second and first cubes.

Jola wants to quit the flower-arranging class.

'It's pointless. What do I need this class for? We don't have any flowers at home. Not even potted plants.'

'We had one, remember? From your mum,' Janek says to comfort his wife, although he's secretly delighted: perhaps now he'll finally be able to buy a steering wheel cover. 'But it died,' he ends sadly, then he shifts his focus to the fifth cube.

'Because I didn't water it. And you forgot about it too,' she says.

Janek gets the fourth ball into the indentation.

'I told you right away that either we should put it in the stairwell so someone else could look after it, or you should take care of it. I'm not good at taking care of plants.'

'And what *are* you good at?'

'This!' Janek hands Jola the cube with all five of its balls in the indentations. 'Watch out!' he yells when the cube slips out of her hand. 'Look what you've done! All that work for nothing!'

'I see you have a new hobby,' Jola says.

'Everyone needs something in life!' Janek snaps at her and leaves the table.

He stands at the window. He does this every time he wants to show his wife that he's offended. In the past, he would smoke a cigarette at the window. Now he just stands with his hands in his pockets and stares out into the darkness. He touches his knees against the radiator. One metal ridge and then the other. He taps out the word 'hobby'. Left knee on 'ho', right on 'bby'. Or should it be 'hob' and 'by'? He would ask Jola, but he won't now because he's offended. He sees the headlights. The airbag expands, the hiss like on a bus before the door closes, his head on the headrest.

'Because of your class, I haven't changed the car's headlight bulbs. If I get a fine tomorrow, you're paying it,' he remarks, but in a joking tone. He wants to defuse the tension.

'They're burned out in my car too. I'll pay both fines,' says Jola, and she goes over to Janek. She embraces him with her right arm and reaches for his hand with her left. She feels the object he's holding. 'Fourth?'

'Fifth,' says Janek with pride, and he starts fiddling with the cube.

Janek wakes up before five. An hour early. He thinks about Bartek. Who was he yelling at? Did his wife go shopping again? He imagines shopaholism. Shopping without any restraint. An impulse that you have to buy something—or else what? A terrible emptiness inside you. Like an alcoholic. Alcoholics need to drink because it's the only thing that'll make them feel okay. The unbearable world will seem better. For a short while. Janek reaches for the sixth. He manipulates the cube in the light from a streetlamp. The sixth cube has a hole in the middle; the balls fall into the second section of it. Such little balls, but they make so much noise. His wife turns on to her side. Janek puts down the cube. He tries to fall asleep.

The engine starts the first time. Janek switches on the headlights. He forgot about the burned-out bulbs. He'll drive slowly. Kuba's coughing. Concerned road users flash their headlights in warning. He doesn't like the term 'road users'. Red. Eighty seconds. He takes out the sixth cube. He's already got three balls in the indentations when he hears honking. He looks up. Green. He steps on the gas and raises his hand in an apologetic gesture. He doesn't reach for the cube at the next traffic light. The sixth one requires focus. He thinks about Bartek. Maybe he'll go over to him and chat a bit. Maybe Bartek needs to talk. He'll get him interested in the Hobby Box. It's something to do. It passes the time, and it also helps improve your concentration. Bartek would finish the first cube right away, and also the second and third. Things would start to get intense with the fourth. And if he showed his wife, maybe it would cure her of shopaholism. When you have a hobby of some kind, a space of your own—Janek doesn't like that word—you feel rejuvenated. It's starting to snow. When the fourth ball falls through the hole, car horns start to honk. Bartek will ask where he can buy a Hobby Box. Or he'll look for it on the Internet. Maybe there are some smaller beginner sets. When a man is burdened with a lot of problems—like Bartek clearly is, since he's been listening to all those recovery testimonials—there's no way he'd want to think about something like the Hobby Box! Janek isn't sure if he'll ever be able to complete the sixth cube. Who invents things like this? It's okay up until the fifth cube, but that hole through which the balls fall into the second section of the sixth cube—it's just too much. It would be a torment to live with someone like that. If Janek had invented the Hobby Box, they would've made a heap of money, but would Jola want to live with someone like that? The airbag, the hiss, his head on the headrest.

10.
Little Cards

The morning sunshine spills into the bedroom through the slits in the blinds. She thinks to herself that this must be how sunlight enters the rooms of those little American motels. She and Jacek have never been to America. They planned it for every milestone anniversary: to hole up in a motel room, lie in bed until noon and wait for breakfast, which would be brought by one of the motel's employees. The hum of air conditioning. But they suddenly lost interest. They forgot all about it, and they're okay with that. Because Jacek is afraid of flying. This kind of light would probably look nice in a photo. Anna reaches for her phone and takes a photo of herself. She's never become comfortable using the word 'selfie'. Unfortunately, she doesn't see in her photo those streaks of light she recalls from photographs in a museum in Berlin—stripes across lovers' bodies, falling through blinds. Not necessarily in a motel. All she sees are the wrinkles on her face. She deletes the photo.

There are flowers on the table and a little card: 'I'll be home in the afternoon.' And a heart with an arrow through it. Anna takes the bouquet out of the vase and hugs it. She gives it a passionate embrace, drenching her nightgown in the process. Like in a film, she thinks. That's how Meryl Streep would embrace flowers. Maybe she did that in *The Hours*? Anna wonders: does Meryl embrace the flowers in that scene at the florist's, or does she just take them out of a bucket? Or maybe it was a metal container… She puts the bouquet back in the vase, but then immediately takes it out again. The stems need trimming. She puts the flowers in the kitchen sink and trims them, one by one. Thirty. When they met, Jacek bought only one flower at a time. After a while, he learned that Anna likes big bouquets. Thirty roses, for example, like in this bouquet. She adjusts the arrangement. When I embrace them like this, it doesn't even hurt, she thinks. She doesn't notice that her finger's bleeding.

She thinks about Fridays; that's when he usually calls her. In her mind, she's already getting in the car. She takes side roads so as not to get caught in any traffic jams, and in ten minutes she's at their favourite café. She imagines him waiting for her in a white suit and hat, with a flower in his buttonhole. She knows it's silly, though, so she never tells him about this foolish daydream. Jacek's an engineer; he works at a construction site. He wears polo shirts and jeans. Never a suit. They sit and have coffee and cake with nut filling. They have a lot to say to each other. They even return to topics they started discussing at breakfast. She likes the beginning of weekends, when Jacek makes time only for her, and after cake and coffee he always gives her a present. For example, he recently gave her a Bill Evans album. One she didn't have yet.

It starts to rain. Anna goes out on to the terrace. A warm, autumn afternoon with subdued sunlight. The lawn needs mowing, Anna thinks. They should do it sometime this week… And then she feels her husband standing behind her.

'It's supposed to rain for two days. Let's wait until the grass dries,' he says.

Jacek and Anna understand each other without speaking. They go into the living room. Jacek smiles and reaches into a drawer of the cupboard they bought while on holiday in Venice. It was so difficult to ship it home. Jacek arranged everything; he spoke with the postmaster. It turned out they had a common passion.

'Guess what it is,' he said joyfully.

Anna answered without hesitation, 'Travel.'

Jacek kisses Anna and she closes her eyes, knowing there's a gift in the drawer. When she opens her eyes, Jacek is already standing next to her again. A burgundy box. A ring. Anna lets Jacek put it on her finger. Bill Evans in the background: *Sunday at the Village Vanguard*. Once, when they were travelling around Spain, Jacek took Anna to a jazz concert. Anna can't remember the pianist's name, but she imagines, while listening to the music with her eyes closed, that she's at that concert of Bill's. She calls him Bill; she allows herself such familiarity because she knows all his albums. They're on a separate shelf and nobody is allowed to put them on the record player except her, and of course Jacek. At that concert the music flows smoothly and Anna listens to Bill with closed eyes; she feels Jacek's hand on her knee, the warm, heavy hand of her engineer, and cigarette smoke tickles her nostrils, but Anna is so close to the real Bill that the smoke doesn't bother her at all because she knows Bill smoked during concerts, and then someone in the audience asks people not to smoke, jarring Anna and making her lose the pulse of the music, and now she doesn't want to listen to this pianist any more, even though he's playing a piece by Bill—'Young and Foolish', from his second album. The ring fits perfectly and has a white stone in it. Anna suggests they open a bottle of wine. They're celebrating their twenty-ninth wedding anniversary. Anna has an art book for Jacek about German modernism. Jacek is fascinated by the works—that's the word he uses—of Max Berg. Every time they visit Wrocław, they go and have a look at the Centennial Hall. They always call it by its German name—*Jahrhunderthalle*. They love to experience its massive splendour. It makes them feel so small and insignificant.

Anna likes receiving little cards for no particular occasion—Jacek leaves them for her in various places. In the shoe cupboard, for example. Just plain little yellow cards with a heart on them. Simple expressions of love and devotion. Once, when a whole week passed without her finding a card, she started to wonder if Jacek had a lover. No, that's stupid, she chastised herself. Then she saw a brand-new set of cards on Jacek's desk, and sighed with relief. The previous set had simply run out. She was happy, but at the same time she grew sad that she had been capable of such a thought. You stupid woman, she berated herself. You've got everything you've ever wanted, but you were ready to question your marriage just because you didn't get a card! She fixes her hair and waits for Jacek—he just pulled into the driveway. The Jaguar's straight from the car wash. As usual before the weekend.

She feels like laughing when she finds a little yellow card inside a box of hot chocolate powder. Anna drinks it every Thursday morning. Jacek is at work then. But he remembered that Thursday mornings are Anna's chocolate time. Anna's heart melts; she sits on the sofa with her legs tucked under her and gazes at the oak tree outside the window. These are the moments of solitude that she needs so much. The moments when you wouldn't be able to call Anna even if there was an emergency, because she puts her phone on silent. She's alone—it's time just for herself. So, Jacek calls her after one o'clock—and Anna tells him how nice it is that he respects her little habits that probably seem ridiculous to others.

'They're the most important things to me!' says Jacek.

Once a week, Anna dusts the upstairs rooms. She has a special duster. You just have to run it over a dirty surface and it shines like new.

'It's like a dust magnet,' she laughs. Jacek ordered it for her from an infomercial. He hires a woman they know for the more serious cleaning. It's better not to touch anything in Jacek's office; there are lots of important sketches and figurines from films everywhere. Jacek has been collecting them for many years. Just for peace of mind, she runs her magic duster along the shelves and the desk. A beep pulls Anna out of her cleaning trance. She searches for the source of the sound. She turns her attention to the package of yellow cards on Jacek's desk.

One card is slightly torn. Did something stop him? Maybe I called him from downstairs? Maybe the phone rang? she wonders. Another sound. There's a tablet lying on his desk. That's where the beep came from. On the screen, it says: 'Wednesday: card and chocolate.'

Anna smiles, remembering last Thursday when she reached for the package of Nesquik and pulled out the yellow card. With a heart on it. She impulsively slides her finger along the screen, and another note appears: 'Friday: coffee, cake.' She slides her finger. 'Wednesday: flowers for Thursday.' She slides it further. 'Friday: coffee, cake, call.' 'Saturday: anniversary next week, find gift.' 'Tuesday: hug.' 'Wednesday: listen to Evans.' 'Monday: reserve tickets.' 'Wednesday: order roses.' 'Friday: tell her she looks lovely.' 'Monday: get home early, flowers.' 'Tuesday: theatre tickets.' 'Wednesday: hug.' 'Friday: suggest going for a walk.' 'Monday: flowers for tomorrow.' 'Wednesday: heart in chocolate.' 'Thursday: call after chocolate.' 'Friday: coffee, cake.' 'Monday: get home early, flowers.' 'Tuesday: film tickets for Thursday.' 'Friday: hug.' 'Wednesday: card in chocolate.' 'Thursday: call after chocolate.' 'Friday: walk on Saturday.' 'Monday: reserve tickets.' 'Wednesday: hug.' 'Thursday: call after chocolate.'

11.
Voices

There's perfect order in Stasia's home. Everything's carefully planned. Coal for the winter was ordered in June, and jars for pickling cucumbers have been waiting on the shelves since May. And her will. Around ten years have already passed since she went to the notary. Only a person with an orderly life dies in peace. Stasia doesn't make any changes to her will, even when her son angrily calls her a religious bigot. And when he dies in a car accident—she leaves it how it is. There are still descendants, after all. It's not good to outlive your own child.

The seamstress visits her on Saturday. The time has come. Stasia says that if you feel they're about to come for you—and you can feel it, if you live a God-fearing life—you need to have your measurements taken so you'll look dignified in the coffin. There's no way round it.

'It won't take much fabric,' Stasia says to the seamstress. 'Look! Skin and bone!' She pinches the skin on her hands, pulling at it and letting it go a few times. It's as grey as packing paper.

But the seamstress doesn't answer. She's annoyed with Stasia because she's a fidgety and impatient client. She'd like to stick a pin in her out of spite.

A week later, it's time to try it on. Stasia looks elegant. She's pleased by her own appearance. She stands in front of the mirror, swaying her hips. She moves like a robot. It's clear she hasn't exercised for a long time; the old bones are reluctant to move. But she's satisfied. She still remembers her first proper dress. A German tailor was making dresses for young women in the area.

Her mood suddenly darkens.

'Add a button! There must be two!' She strokes the jacket's fabric.

There's a stern look on her face.

The seamstress picks up the suit and turns to leave.

'Two buttons! Who's ever heard of that?' she suddenly snaps as she reaches the door. 'Either one or three!'

The seamstress wishes she could slam the door. She'll be back after Christmas, because now she's leaving town for the holidays.

To think of her wedding dress and not pull the album out of her cupboard—impossible. Stasia looks for her wedding photo. It's behind the portraits of Grażyna and Danusia, her friends from middle school. She runs her finger across her husband's face. He's been gone from this world for so many years. She has forgotten his voice. She puts her ring finger on Antek and closes her eyes. She imagines one of those moments—one of the last ones, a typical scene. Antek is sitting in the bathtub. Stasia leans over him. Antek instructs: 'Lower, oh, here, here!' They washed each other's backs every Saturday. Stasia says it out loud, trying to recreate his voice: 'Oh, here, here, lower, oh, here, lower…' But she can't find the right tone. One time she says the word 'lower' in such a way that it makes her smile.

'Lower, lower, oh, here…' Eventually, she starts to feel sorry for Antek because the water's cold. She opens her eyes. It's 1972, and the priest's words in the cemetery are drowned out by a passing train.

After New Year's Day, the jacket has a second button. Stasia's delighted. The seamstress is happy too, because she doesn't like getting behind in her work. And she no longer feels as annoyed at her client as before. They'll settle up and that's the last Stasia will ever see of her.

'The sleeves are too long. They cover half my hands!'

'They'll be fixed in the coffin, Madam,' says the seamstress.

'Maybe they will, maybe they won't—will I have a say in that?'

'And have you bought a grave? And chosen a coffin?'

'Of course. Last summer I paid for another twenty years.'

'But you still can't be sure that's where you'll be laid to rest!'

'The sleeves are too long,' Stasia says, unconvinced. 'Correct them!' She remembers the painter who renovated their apartment. Antek took him to task before settling the bill. He showed him that the corners were sloppy and there was still a bit of old paint on the wall, behind the radiator. But Stasia can't hear her husband's voice. She can only see him in her mind's eye pointing out the imperfections with a broomstick.

The seamstress takes the jacket and leaves the room without saying another word. Stasia goes to the window. She looks out at the foul winter weather. Soon there'll be more sunlight and the days will be longer. But she doesn't have much time left. The measurements have been taken but the suit isn't ready; she feels worried. She hides behind the curtain because the seamstress has gone out into the yard. She's walking, then she speeds up, then she glances back at Stasia's window—oh, how she wishes she could throw a stone at it!

A lot of time passes but the seamstress doesn't return. And she doesn't answer her phone! This exhausts Stasia. At this age, you never know. She calls again and again, even in the evenings, but no one answers. Stasia doesn't know what to do. She takes out a suitcase full of summer clothes and looks for an outfit to wear in the coffin. Suddenly the doorbell rings. It's the seamstress. She was a bit ill, but the work is done. The sleeves have been shortened and there are even two buttons on each sleeve, for symmetry.

'There was only one button on each sleeve before,' she says, reminding Stasia of the situation before Christmas.

But Stasia is not consoled. Her husband's voice keeps bothering her.

'Do you remember Antek?'

'Sure, why wouldn't I?' remarks the seamstress with feigned indifference.

'He went hunting with your husband.'

'I remember you accusing us of cheating you out of boar meat.'

'If you remember such things, perhaps you remember Antek's voice?'

The seamstress sits down on the sofa. She squints, and now she can see Antek. Yes, she remembers him well. He was quite agreeable, and not very argumentative. Unlike Stasia.

'His voice?' she asks.

'Yes… The kind of voice he had.'

'Well, I don't remember,' the seamstress responds, thinking about it. 'The kind of voice… Well, he had a masculine voice.'

'Never mind,' says Stasia. 'Show me the suit.'

Stasia puts on the skirt. It fits her perfectly. And the jacket isn't bad either. It just reeks of cigarette smoke because the seamstress is a chain-smoker. But Stasia doesn't want to reproach her any more. She wants the seamstress to go away and leave her in peace. It's such a gloomy day that she just wants to lie down in bed. It's probably why the neighbours stopped taking their clothes to her. Because of the cigarettes.

It's nice work, Stasia thinks. In the old days, people had solid trades. They could make a good living if they knew their craft well. Not like now, when everyone is a bungler; she shudders while thinking of her neighbour, who hasn't been able to repair his tap for a whole year. One day, the dripping sound will drive Stasia to her grave.

'Please hold the mirror behind me,' she says to the seamstress. Stasia takes the mirror from the dresser.

'Why are you waving it around like that? It's not a paintbrush! Stop it!' Stasia snaps.

The seamstress's hands have gone numb because the mirror is heavy. She holds her elbows against her chest to support the weight.

'It hangs badly at the back. Fix it!' says Stasia in a sharp tone, and she sees her husband in her mind: he's arguing with a mechanic about the car. He knows a lot about it, he's lain under that car many times himself, but some things just can't be taken care of on one's own. 'Fix it!' she tells the seamstress again, louder and more emphatically. It makes a shiver run down her back.

And the seamstress leaves, but she doesn't take the suit with her. She shuts the door, but then she opens it again in order to slam it with all her might. Stasia runs after the seamstress, but she's already on the ground floor. Stasia goes back inside the apartment, stands by the window and struggles with the handle. She's angry that she didn't let Antek talk her into replacing the windows. The seamstress walks through the yard and then disappears behind the neighbouring apartment building. And then Stasia thinks—no, she's certain—that she hears a voice saying, 'Easy now, easy. Don't worry.' Antek's voice. A hoarse voice, slightly reedy. Stasia hangs the suit on the door, so it'll be in clear view.

It's the end of January. The seamstress is lying in a coffin. Stasia approaches the altar in tiny steps. The man in front of her—not only is he tall, blocking her view of the entire church, he's walking unsteadily as well, wobbling from side to side. Either he'll stop suddenly and I'll crash into him, or he'll fall over and I'll trip over him, Stasia thinks. Unnecessary trouble. So she stops. She waits a moment. The man places his hand on the seamstress's forehead. Stasia can only see her nose; people's noses stick out so prominently after they die, as if all their deceit has escaped along with their souls. Now she's standing next to the coffin. She looks inside. There are two buttons on the jacket.

12.
He Also Once Stayed in a Small Cabin

Smiling with a set of perfectly even teeth, the man catches their attention while they're looking for a parking spot. His white shorts and shirt accentuate his tan—a sign of health and success. The man is standing next to a Mercedes. He's writing something in a notebook and leaning against the car door. One elbow is resting on the mirror. They park their old Opel next to him. Graceful legs, for a man. And strong hands, but not the hands of a worker, the mother thinks. Moleskine, thinks the delighted daughter, torn from a daydream about attending a creative writing course. Turbo version, the father thinks, nodding with appreciation as he admires the air intakes behind the front wheel arches. It's impossible not to notice them. Everyone climbs out of the Opel. Carefully, so as not to bang the door against the sleek body of the car with the star on its hood.

'Camping?' the man remarks, but he immediately apologises for his casual tone, which the mother likes very much because it confirms her theory about the ordinariness of great people—those who have found success at a mature age.

'Indeed!' the father eagerly responds, which upsets the mother and daughter. They don't like it when he uses old-fashioned language, which in his mind expresses deference towards the interlocutor.

'A long way…' the mother begins, and then she glances up at the cloudless sky. 'But it was worth it!'

'I come here every year. I've never been disappointed. My name's Jurek!' The man stretches out his hand and greets them in the appropriate order, ending with the father.

The man's use of the first-person singular instead of the first-person plural is very conspicuous. So conspicuous, in fact, that one has to restrain oneself from asking why he comes here by himself, since he's such a handsome and, by all appearances, successful man. But the mother knows this isn't a good question—he might think she's a nosy woman. She'll find out eventually. She'll give herself some time; they've only just arrived, and have the entire holiday ahead of them. But she's surprised at herself for thinking so hopefully about it. After all, she's married, and last week she and the father had very good sex, she recalls. Although she's not fond of that term. *We made love*, she corrects herself in her mind, then she opens the boot of the car.

Jurek is wearing sunglasses with gold frames. The daughter has a pair like that, too, but she left them in the car. It would be silly for her to climb back into the car now in order to put them on. After all, anyone can have sunglasses like these—unless Jurek's are Ray-Bans. She got hers at the bazaar for twenty-five złoty; there's no point parading such cheap knock-offs. She glances into the boot. It smells like rissoles. She and the mother spent a whole day frying them before the trip. Oh, how out of place they are here: she, the mother and the father, with their baggage crammed into their old Opel and their carefully packed two weeks' worth of supplies. Jurek most likely eats in restaurants or even takes a motorboat to the island, where scantily clad waitresses serve calamari, the daughter thinks. She shuts the boot, nearly slamming it on the mother's hand.

'Hey, be careful!' the mother shrieks, but she immediately changes her tone of voice and the final word—'careful'—sounds gentle, maybe even comical, more like maternal scolding than resentment. She glances around for Jurek and the father.

They're standing next to the Mercedes. Their heads are lowered. Typical, thinks the mother. Men tend to lower their heads when standing next to a car. Nevertheless, this typical pose makes her feel more closely connected to Jurek. The men are discussing the turbo lag.

'According to Wikipedia, this phenomenon is the result of a delay between the momentary exhaust output and the air demand at a given moment, in undetermined conditions of engine operation,' says Jurek. 'It results from the inertia of the turbocharger rotor and the gas-dynamic connection between the turbocharger unit and the engine,' he concludes.

'And what's yours like, Jurek?' the father asks.

'It varies,' replies Jurek casually. 'It's an old, well-preserved 124, but I haven't had it very long, so I don't yet have the feel for it a professional would. You can't have a feel for everything!' He smiles, and his teeth sparkle in the sun.

Tears well up in the father's eyes. Fortunately, he's wearing his sunglasses. Not like Jurek's. Ordinary plastic ones.

The ones he wears when he rides his bike. He feels like crying because the owner of a nearly antique Mercedes—a man towards whom he initially felt antipathy because it didn't even occur to him that such a person could ever be interested in him—unexpectedly reveals his weakness to him: he admits that he doesn't know how to drive a turbocharged car. And he talks about it frankly, without ostentation, so the father sticks his fingers under the lenses of his sunglasses and, as if scratching himself, wipes away his tears. He thinks he could make friends with Jurek, share the joys and sorrows of married life with him, talk about cars and occasionally go out for a beer.

'You'll tame this beast before long!' he consoles Jurek, touching a tyre with his foot. 'Fulda! The king of tyres!'

'Why not queen?' asks the daughter.

'That's right!' Jurek praises the daughter. 'The king is Dunlop!'

Their cabin is modest but well maintained. The father and mother flop on to the wide double bed and lie there for a while. They stare at the ceiling. There's a crack that starts at the overhead light and winds gracefully towards the window. There, at the end of the black line, sits a spider. The mother grabs the father's hand. He stands up lazily, grasps one of his flip-flops and, jumping, hits the ceiling with it. He misses. Another jump. He misses. He reaches for a chair. He climbs up on it. He's so close to the spider that the next strike will surely be fatal.

'What are you doing?!' the daughter screams. 'Don't kill it!'

The parents give the daughter a reproachful look. The father gently knocks the spider down with his flip-flop and the spider runs behind the bed.

'I'm not sleeping here!' the mother screams. 'You can sleep with the spiders yourself!'

The kitchen is small, but well equipped. There are pots, a few cups and cutlery. They didn't need to bring their own from home, wrapped in newspaper. There's even a sandwich toaster. The mother raises the lid—not even scorched—but she wipes it with a cloth anyway, for peace of mind.

The living room is modest and cosy. As agreed in advance, there's no TV. Two armchairs and a sofa, perfect for an evening rest. The mother sits down on the sofa and checks its firmness. She looks up at the ceiling. Clean. No cracks or spiders.

'We'll definitely get a good rest here,' she remarks, and then she goes to the bedroom to unpack the suitcases.

The wardrobes look spacious; they haven't brought many things anyway. For dinner they'll go to a restaurant. That's what they promised themselves before they left—they'd eat out on the first and last evening.

A few minutes before seven o'clock, they're ready. The father: light-coloured trousers and a white polo shirt. He slides his finger across the logo with the rider on a horse. A friend once told him that if the shirt is genuine, the horse should be facing left. He looks at his pale hands, and at the scratches the cat left on them. Last weekend, the father came home after drinking with some friends. The cat started playing around. It clung to his hand, scratching and biting. When a man is drunk, he gives up. The next day—his hand was all red, as if he'd dragged it through shattered glass. But where had the glass come from? the father wonders while waiting for the mother. A white dress on her tanned body. Nowadays, tanning salons aren't as harmful as they used to be. The same goes for microwave ovens. If only that gold chain with a cross wasn't hanging between her breasts... No, he won't start again. He doesn't want a row on the very first day of their holiday. The daughter: black shorts and a linen blouse. Her black bra is too visible through her blouse, the father thinks, but no, he won't start again. He doesn't want a row on the first day of their holiday.

'Good evening!' Jurek suddenly appears in front of the father. 'Are you settled in? May I?' He walks into the cabin and glances around the living room. 'I stayed in cabins like this when I first started coming here,' he says. 'Now I stay at the end of the campsite. It's quieter there.'

'More expensive?' the father asks.

'The cabin is larger, so it's more expensive,' Jurek laughs. 'You're welcome to come round for a drink in the evening!' And then he calls out in the direction of the mother, who's in the midst of fixing her hair: 'Bye!'

'Bye!' answers the mother, and then she immediately looks in the mirror. She checks how she looked at the moment when he said 'bye' to her. Acceptable.

They choose Italian food. The mother loves pizza, the father loves pizza and the daughter also loves pizza. A double crust with double cheese. The mother glances at her stomach—before she left, the dress fitted her perfectly. Now it looks tight. I'll just suck it in, she thinks, but she quickly chastises herself; after all, she's on holiday, so why is she behaving as if she were at a fashion show? And not so long ago she thought she was finally free of all this and no longer gave a damn—not a damn!—about her appearance. Just as long as she doesn't go too far and, for example, let herself get fat. The parents agree: the daughter can drink a glass of wine. But they won't squeeze in dessert—even if they get it for free. The father takes out a credit card and turns it between his thumb and forefinger. The mother and daughter look at the card, then at him.

'Plastic money,' says the father.

'So...?' The daughter looks at the father, looks him straight in the eyes in the same way he looks at her after parent–teacher meetings.

'Convenience,' he says, unsure of his own words.

A tip has been added to the bill, to which the father agrees by clicking the word 'yes' on the terminal.

'How was it?' Jurek suddenly appears in front of them as they're saying goodbye to the waiter.

They say—in unison—that it was delicious, that they've never had better pizza in their lives, well, maybe they have, but on holiday, with the sea in the background, it tastes different, but having the tip hidden in the terminal... It forces the customer to decide quickly, in the waiter's presence, whether to give one or not. And it's impossible to refuse.

'It's not like it used to be. A tip was an unguaranteed reward for service, it was personal, it was for the waiter who exerted some effort, who tried hard to ensure that nothing was lacking, like…' the father's voice trails off for a moment, 'Marek Kondrat in *Hotel Pacific*! That's my idea of perfect service!'

'I don't know,' says the mother. 'I wouldn't want to work for a boss like Wilhelmi.'

'I'm not talking about the back office,' the father shoots back. 'I mean the overall image of the restaurant, an institution based on respect for the customer, for the consumer, a place that's… traditional!'

'When did you become such a traditionalist?' laughs the mother. She would point out the father's hypocrisy to him, if Jurek weren't there.

'It's not about that,' says the father. 'It's about the tip. But never mind!' he breaks off. He would get cross with the mother, if Jurek weren't there.

'Well, I'd like to invite you to my place,' Jurek says to the father and mother. 'The young lady, too.'

The daughter's cheeks turn red. She lowers her gaze and stares at her evenly trimmed toenails. 'Thank you,' she says, then she curtsies and slips her arm under the mother's arm.

His house—under no circumstances could it be called a 'cabin'—is situated on a hill among pine trees. Narrow steps lead up to it. The mother is uncomfortable with the fact that—being invited to go first—she'll be ascending the steps in front of Jurek. Jurek could go last, but the father allows their host to go ahead of him, of course, so the mother climbs up the steps and feels that her underwear isn't positioned as it should be, it's cutting into the crack between her butt cheeks, but it's too late to fix it because in this situation it would be very unsightly. The ascent is long, her underwear is cutting deeper and deeper, and now the mother is seriously regretting that she doesn't wear thongs, that she isn't keen on those little strings that go between the buttocks. If she were wearing one now, she wouldn't have to expose Jurek to a sight like this. However, such a well-bred man surely walks with a lowered gaze, for he knows that the daughter is behind him and the father bringing up the rear, completely unaware of what his wife is going through right now. They arrive at the terrace. This is where they'll sit.

'It's so beautiful here!' the mother exclaims. 'What a view!' Her gaze sweeps across the sea, the boats swaying on it and the yachts resting in the small marina.

'I book it for one month every year. This is the only place where I can truly relax.'

They sit down at a table with massive legs and a thick top—under no circumstances could it be called a typical 'garden table'. Jurek asks them to wait a moment and leaves the mother, father and daughter. They sit silently. It's quieter here, more private. Far from the noise of the lower campsite. And the view! The crowns of the trees conceal what's below. You can get away from everything, disconnect, forget about it all, thinks the mother. Emigrate inwardly. But he also once stayed in a small cabin, she reassures herself. And this beautiful green carpet looks as if it was woven by thousands of little hands, ponders the daughter, gazing at the trees. However, she quickly gets a grip on herself because she went too far, imagining little children slaving away for a bowl of rice. That's not what her novel will be like; that's not how she's going to describe the setting.

'Ta-da!' Jurek appears in the doorway leading to the terrace, pushing in front of him a minibar on wheels. The father expertly assesses the contents: sparse, but classy. A decent whisky, an anisette and a jug of well-cooled water, judging by the frosted glass, as well as two bottles of beer and white wine in a decanter.

'For smokers, there are chocolate cigarillos… almost like in *Hydrozagadka*!' Jurek laughs.

'An excellent film!' the daughter exclaims, jumping to her feet. 'Ace is my hero!'

'*Take off your hat!*' the father exclaims, jumping to his feet.

'*Herman!*' the mother shrieks.

'*Feuer!*' Jurek concludes the exchange.

He hit the bull's-eye. After just an hour together, they're already at the stage that's usually only reached after several days of social banter.

The mother chooses wine while the father and Jurek decide to drink beer, to cool off. The daughter, with the silent consent of her parents, decides to have some anisette. Everything is pleasant.

'It'll be such a shame to go back,' says the mother, and she stops the rim of her glass right in front of her mouth. She has recently seen a photo of an actress in a similar pose. She thinks she looks attractive.

'Once,' the father begins, 'when I was in primary school, I bit through a glass at a friend's birthday party. I was so stressed out!'

'The same thing happened to me!' Jurek says, reaching for his glass. 'Fortunately I wasn't injured.'

The mother moves the glass away from her mouth. A trace of lipstick.

'What do you do for a living, Jurek?' she asks. 'Sorry to be so direct… But, you know, a woman's curiosity. You don't have to tell us, of course.'

'I'm a dental technician!'

'Well, now I know how you got that pearly smile!' the mother laughs and reaches for a cigarillo. 'Do you mind?' Her fingers hover a few millimetres from the packet.

'You don't smoke!' The father sets down his glass of beer.

'Just one…' the mother says, leaning towards Jurek. The flame from the silver Zippo trembles in the wind. 'It's obvious at first glance! Such teeth! Healthy and strong!'

Jurek picks up the bottle of whisky. He exchanges a knowing glance with the father.

'They're implants.' He taps his upper incisors with his fingernail. 'A gift from my wife for my fiftieth birthday.'

The silence is awkward and tiresome. Especially for the mother, who has just taken a puff from the cigarillo and is blowing smoke over her shoulder. What did she expect? That such a man would be an old bachelor? That he had somehow remained single all this time? That he was perhaps divorced? What was I hoping for? she wonders, and she glances at the father's crooked teeth.

'Oh, so you're married?' she finally says.

'For twenty years. My wife gave birth in March, so she's staying home with the baby… And she gave me the traditional month off.'

'She's all alone with the baby?' the daughter asks.

'Not alone. With her sister and a nanny. She'll manage.'

'A brave woman,' says the daughter, and finishes off her glass of anisette.

'I'll be seeing them very soon; I'm going home tomorrow night! So, let's drink to our pleasant meeting!'

The conversation flows with the right rhythm, touching on broader and increasingly intimate topics. Jurek tells them about his teeth, which caused him trouble when he was younger, and about the tonnes of antibiotics given to him by his parents when he had even the slightest infection. He talks about his profession, his job in a medium-sized city in southern Poland, the firm he runs by himself and the dental office he owns with his brother. He expounds upon the comfort of having implants and assures them that nothing lifts a person's spirits like knowing it's possible to say 'no' to tooth decay once and for all.

The mother looks at Jurek. She gazes boldly at his strong, white teeth. How well they must grind meat, how thoroughly they must shred it before it reaches the stomach. And how much less work the stomach has to do in order for that meat, even the rarest steak, to enter the body in the form of valuable elements. How these implants can improve one's health! She touches her own repeatedly patched teeth with her tongue. All healthy, but only for the time being. She reaches, without asking, for another cigarillo.

Jurek brings a bowl of salad. And cutlery—much larger than in the cabin down below. The mother thinks she's never seen such large cutlery before! Jurek deftly impales lettuce leaves with his fork and puts them in his mouth full of even teeth. Food is broken down very efficiently in there. It's a grinding machine. A reliable shredding mechanism. How much pure grace and pleasure there is when eating with teeth like those! The crunching that accompanies this activity seems to echo all the way to the beach.

And the daughter tries to imagine what it's like to kiss the owner of tooth implants. She wonders if they're as smooth as porcelain. Or maybe they'd feel like tinted glass? They have some decorative bottles at home. She hates having to dust them before Christmas. Would she like to kiss Jurek? She slides her glass towards him, but the father signals to her that she's had enough. He wonders how much implants might cost. The mother—judging by her facial expression and the way her tongue is moving restlessly along her upper and lower jaws—would like to get some for herself. But they're planning to buy a new car in the spring. At the annual clearance sale.

On the way home from their holiday—it went by so quickly, but they got some rest, which is the main thing—the mother has a dream. She's leaving work; it's a June evening, the air is fresh. I'll walk home, it'll do me good, she thinks. She strolls along light-heartedly, reminiscing about the carefree days of her youth when she would return home from school after the diplomas had been handed out. And there's the pre-summer excitement: holidays, warm earth, lying in the grass and waiting for a brief rainstorm. Then, suddenly, strong hands pull her into the doorway of an old apartment building slated for demolition and, by pressing on the lumbar region of her spine, paralyse her. But she remains conscious. Then the same hands place a metal frame over her head, the front part of which enters her mouth. The hands, already in latex gloves and armed with something resembling pliers, start unscrewing implants—one by one. The sound of teeth being thrown into a bowl. One, two, three. The mother wakes up and grabs the father's hand. He brakes violently.

The car comes to a standstill, diagonally across the road. A van approaching from the opposite direction stops right in front of the Opel's bonnet. The daughter raises her head: strong headlights are shining straight into her face. The car's interior is suddenly lit up, exposing stains and spots on the ceiling, traces of many years of use, even though nobody sits on the ceiling or touches it. They can't even eat a sandwich in the car. The mother touches her face and checks for blood.

'I'm sorry,' the father says. He switches on the hazard lights and tries to get the car back into the right lane.

13.
The Pit

My father's eyesight is very weak. The things he looks at blur together, get chopped up, and split in half. The parts slide in opposite directions like cherries on a slot machine. Up and down. But he still drives his taxi. Twice a week, when the traffic's lighter. He drives so he won't completely deteriorate. He says: 'It's easy to deteriorate, but hard to rejuvenate.' On those occasions, I follow him in my car. God knows what the old man's going to do. In a business like this, you've got to be careful. I keep my finger on the pulse. He used to lead me through this world, but now I'm his guardian. Incognito. If he knew, he'd stop driving. And deteriorate. Neither of us wants that. Like rats. We don't want them, either. At the car workshop, there are two large pits. The rats sit inside pipes and scurry from one pit to the other. It spooks me out.

He drives slowly. The light's on inside his car. I look at his Audi—it's like an ambulance. He's a spry old guy. He gesticulates at who knows whom, filling the car with his presence. At the corner of Piłsudskiego Street he crosses over to the left lane and I follow him, but he cuts back into the right lane just before he reaches the traffic lights. Our cars are side by side now. My father fiddles with the radio. He raises his head and strains his eyes. He looks at the lights.

I see his profile, his sharp nose. He glances to his left. He squints. Then he fiddles with the radio again.

People call him 'Camel'. Because of the cigarettes. In the 1980s, hardly anyone could get Camels. And my father really liked them. In a soft pack, without filters. Camels or nothing. He could go a whole week without smoking when there weren't any Camels at the Pewex shop. And when they showed up, he'd take five packets right away. Then he'd hang around with his friends and share his Camels with them—generously, without worrying that he'd run out. They took long drags, savouring the flavour, and smoked each cigarette to the very end. I stayed near my father all the time in those days, like a pathetic puppy dog.

He stops at Poprzeczna Street. A man in an overcoat gets in his car. The light goes out. They sit together, very still. My father switches on the light. The man gets out. He raises his hand in farewell.

The city is deserted. We're alone together, at a safe distance. Sometimes I take a friend with me, because driving is always better with company. We talk about this and that, meandering from one topic to the next. Engines, for example—Adrian knows nothing about diesel, he's driven on petrol his whole life. And women—we both have good relationships with our women because we stay out of each other's way. Then Adrian says he's never been stuck in such a bad traffic jam in his life. I look—it's a taxi stand. When Adrian and I chat, we really get absorbed. After a while, Monika calls to say she's leaving. I lose sight of the old man.

I follow my father and think about how the younger generation doesn't have that kind of perseverance to try to make it in life. He achieved what he wanted to achieve. And he didn't hurt anybody. Only flies. He can really swat those bastards! What an eye! They fall one by one. I can't even kill a mosquito. Blood disgusts me. I knock them down with my hand. He stops on Żeromskiego Street. A girl gets in. They drive away. My father's no ladies' man. After my mum died, he didn't get involved with anyone. Did he visit whores? I don't think so. A Catholic mourns for the rest of his life. There are photos of my mum hanging everywhere at home; sometimes I can't look at them. When my father dies, I'll put all those holiday snapshots away in a drawer. And the ones taken at family parties. And my First Communion. I'll leave only their wedding photo on the wall. They stop. The girl gets out and says something to my father through the window. She gives him her hand. An endearing old man. Charming. A signet ring with a ruby on his little finger. His finger has swollen so much that you can't pull it off. My father will take the ring with him to his grave. People seem to lose weight in old age and their clothes start to hang on them like on a scarecrow, but their bodies also swell in certain spots. My father is aging asymmetrically. His skin hangs off his hands, but his belly sticks out. And his chest is sunken. He has something in common with John Paul II: he's not ashamed of old age. But he didn't want to lie on the beach in a Speedo when we went to the seaside.

'I'm not going to make a fool of myself and freak people out,' he said.

The cult of the body no longer exists. Fatties flaunt themselves freely. And that's good. If someone doesn't like it, they don't have to look. People have other problems. More serious ones. Like when the sump bursts and you have to go down into the pit and the rats are there. They arch their tails and stare at you with those beady little eyes. And when they're backed into a corner, maybe they'll even jump right at your throat—you never know. The light inside my father's car is malfunctioning. It's starting to flicker. Now it's no longer an ambulance, but a mobile disco. I feel like laughing because that flashing will make my father go completely blind. I told him during the summer to take the Audi to an electrician.

'I'm not going to let some bungler mess around with the ceiling of my car,' my father said. He taps the light. It stops flickering. We start driving again.

Końcowa Street. Two guys and a girl. I need to focus. They get in. The light goes off and on again. I drive closer to him. You never know what young punks like that will get up to. Once my father kicked a teenager out of his car who insisted on lighting a cigarette and blowing the smoke out the window.

'It's completely out of the question,' my father told him.

And the guy said my father wouldn't notice anything because they were just slim menthol cigarettes. And that he doesn't even notice the smoke himself, while he's smoking them. My father asked him why he smoked, then, if he doesn't notice the smoke.

'Just to keep my hands busy,' the guy answered, thinking he'd managed to win the old man over. As soon as he'd lit it, my father attacked him with pepper spray. One smoker crossed off the list. You just don't do that to people. It's completely out of the question.

The boys get out. The girl stays. They drive away. That was stressful. On the radio, they're reading something. I like listening to books. The reader's voice has a good effect on me. Someone who reads literature on the radio for a living needs to have self-discipline. They have to sit for hours at a time in the studio, and they can't make any mistakes while reading. And they have to read it dramatically enough so that the listener won't get bored. I have audiobooks in the glovebox. I like them too. I've recently been listening to *The Doll* by Bolesław Prus. And I have to say that I wouldn't wish a girl like Łęcka on anyone. To mistreat someone like that—for what reason? Ancestry? And Stanisław lets himself be treated that way. I feel sorry for him. He's a good capitalist and very determined, like my father. He can predict trends. Sure, he made some money during the war. So what? Everyone finds ways of making money. Just as long as you don't have a direct hand in someone else's misery. But I don't even know any more. There are no rules in war. But Rzecki—the spitting image of my father. Calm and collected.

The difference, though, is that my father plays the accordion. The concerts he used to give! All the tenants of our building would get together on New Year's Eve. My father and a neighbour would play together. All the old hits. The neighbour sang and kept rhythm on a tambourine. No vodka, because he had to drive. I remember my mum clapping and hopping about, but she refused to dance with anyone, even Zyga. She said she wanted to dance with my father first. And he played on and on, right to the very end, just like on the *Titanic*. There used to be order in the world. Basic principles. My father would laugh and say, 'Don't worry about it, just dance!' I saw them dance together once. During a dance party at Parkowa. A friend and I watched through the window. My father's large hand was on my mum's back, just above her bottom. I felt safe. He was very polite, well bred. No public groping. I don't do that, either. I never embarrassed Monika in front of people. Nor in private. But she couldn't stand the tension. People sometimes can't. I understand that. I'm tense myself, sometimes. But I don't feel it as strongly now that I'm alone. One becomes immune eventually.

Żytnia Street. No customers. The light is on. Waiting is the worst. When one waits like this, various thoughts come to mind. One starts remembering things. Like when the number on the odometer started with a one, not a five. Things were good then, because engine repairs were still in the distant future. And petrol was so cheap… And so one sits and thinks. And one loses the will to live. But then a customer usually appears and the thoughts dissipate. Such is the way of this world that salvation comes when it is needed most. But not everyone is that lucky. My father's friend hanged himself in his cellar. The worst is when people with no family or friends take their own lives. It's a problem for doctors when they find a hanged man after a lot of time has passed. But I guess they've seen everything. If you've pulled a kid out of a barrel, you won't be afraid of hell itself.

Still no customers. Half an hour gone to waste. We drive away. Eleven o'clock. They've shut the traffic lights off. My father accelerates. If you drive ten kilometres per hour in a traffic jam, and then suddenly accelerate to fifty, you get pressed back into your seat. My father really liked to gun it in the old days. After he bought the one-year-old Audi, we went for a drive outside the city. And we hit one-eighty! He was a good driver. Confident. In gloves that had belonged to the car's original German owner, which he found in the glovebox. They fitted so well it was as if they'd been made for him. We flew through the forest, passing sign after sign warning motorists of wild animals jumping into the road.

'I've never seen so many signs in the same place,' I said. And my father started telling me about my grandfather, a hunter, and how one time he was unable to pull the trigger. A roe deer was in his rifle scope: full-grown and handsome. In communist times, even the deer were skinny, but this one looked like it had just eaten breakfast. It was walking through the grove, looking around. Young, curious about the world. And suddenly their eyes met: my grandfather's eye in the rifle scope and hers there, far away in the grove. And this roe deer looked at my grandfather; it moved its head, and a tear trickled down from its eye. One tear, then another one. Tears as big as peas. Grandpa started to cry, and he lowered his rifle. He never went hunting again... 'And he even became a vegetarian,' said my father, though he immediately added that sausages kept disappearing from the fridge. At least, my grandmother complained that they disappeared. It takes a strong emotional experience to make a person understand. When Monika left me, I cried. And then I understood. We haven't remained friends, as is fashionable nowadays. We don't call each other. I saw her once at the grocer's, waiting at the cash desk next to mine. Clearly shopping for the weekend, since she had a lot of stuff. She paid by card. And I guess it was declined because she put her groceries back in the trolley and headed into the aisles. I waited at the exit; when she came out, she wasn't carrying any bags. If she'd called me, I would've helped. I'm the type of person that likes to help others. One of my neighbours from the ground floor, Zyga's grandson, comes round asking for change so he can buy cigarettes. I always give him some, and afterwards I always forget that I have. And once he surprised me by stopping by my place to pay off his debt.

Klasztorna Street. A priest gets in. They drive away. How do priests' bellies get so huge? It's usually the ones with seniority. Thankfully the Audi is spacious; the priest had no trouble climbing in. But he wouldn't be able to fit in the tiny car Monika's sister bought. Lots of praying, not much exercise. Or some kind of genetic predisposition. Genes affect the brain, so maybe the connection is that those with a tendency to be overweight decide to become priests. It's different when it comes to nuns—in any case, they don't drive around. They have no money. The Mother Superior takes everything. My cousin's friend is a nun. She gets pocket money from her parents who live in the countryside; they're farmers, with one hundred hectares of land.

And everything they send to her vanishes. The poor girl walks around in sandals until autumn. Then she gets sick. And that's the life of a nun, completely pointless. A priest doesn't have to reckon with anyone except the bishop. But it's a totally different story when it comes to bishops—different bellies. I won't comment on them, though, because I don't know any.

He's crawling along again. Forty-five. Maybe the load's too heavy? It's amusing. I recognise this priest by the bag he's carrying. He usually gives my father a couple of holy pictures as he leaves. My father sticks them in the gap at the base of his window. Saint Joseph, the Polish Pope, and three different pictures of Saint Hubert. One time, the police stopped him. My father made the sign of the cross over the pictures and then said, raising his hands towards the car roof, 'Praise the Lord!' They left him in peace. So I don't give my father a hard time about those pictures or try to convince him to take them down. If they bring him luck, they can stay.

They've been driving for a long time, for a trip with a priest. Now they're almost on the outskirts. I call my father. He doesn't answer. His light's flickering. The shopping centre is on the right. My father accelerates. I call again. Eighty on the speedometer. Something must have happened. They turn into a side street. I switch off my headlights. They park. It's bright in the cab. My father looks like he's leaning towards the priest, and his head is down. I'm not worried, since it's a priest, but I'm still a bit anxious. The priest gets out and lights a cigarette. My father does, too.

They stand on either side of the Audi with their backs to each other. My father goes over to the priest and embraces him. They hug for a long time. I drive away.

Once, when we were standing by those pits filled with rats, my father told me that if a woman embraces a woman, it means there's a problem that needs to be solved.

'But a man embraces another man,' he said, throwing a wad of crumpled paper at a rat, 'when a problem has been solved. That's what differentiates us.'

14.
The Light of Life

This song is on the radio all the time. Even a nice melody gets boring when they play it over and over again, Halinka thinks. But not this one! She's happy when she hears it coming over the radio a few minutes past six. She goes to the bathroom, splashes her face with cold water and glances at her reflection in the mirror. There are dark bags under her eyes from lack of sleep.

Forty years old, but Halinka's beauty still impresses her friends. Her husband, less so. He's so accustomed to Halinka's youthful appearance that he no longer notices it. Not like her friends. 'Halinka, your beauty is eternal, and that golden hair… you'll never go grey, and if you do, nobody will notice. Just don't cut it,' they advise her. 'Grow old with dignity. Accept your age.'

Halinka accepts it, but the dark bags are there. She goes to the kitchen to boil some water for tea, porridge, and coffee for Stefek, who's still asleep even though yesterday he offered to get up earlier than usual this morning. He often says that, but he works hard and gets home late. There's a difference in their income levels, so she tries to be helpful, though she would also love to sleep in until nine o'clock.

'Throw away all the bad things in life,' Halinka sings and hums along to the radio, while slicing bread for sandwiches.

She spreads butter on the slices of bread and lays lettuce leaves on them evenly so that they won't stick out, so that the sandwiches will be aesthetically pleasing… But if they aren't, so what?! she thinks, getting irritated with herself momentarily, then laughing it off.

Maybe she should throw all this away? she wonders, and this plan unexpectedly starts to gain significance. There are moments when such ideas become meaningful. It's been a very long time since she had any plans apart from what to make for breakfast, lunch and dinner. And this sudden plan is so vivid in her mind—like never before. There have been times when she thought of changing something in her life, but that was long ago. When she was still at university. She barely remembers those days.

Maybe she could leave and start a new life? No, not alone. She wouldn't be able to get by on her own. Although who knows… Images flutter through her mind and a warm sensation starts to fill her abdomen. One of her friends uses dating websites, but once she ended up in a bar with a bad date: he drank four beers and then had a double shot of vodka at the counter. He stood with his back to her, but she could see he was drinking. Then he couldn't utter a single word. So if she's going to throw everything away, it'll be with her husband and children, without taking any risks. But they'll have to go far away—far from this city with its traffic jams and concrete, far from the grind, and buy a cottage in the countryside, even a run-down one in need of renovation, where they'll be able to enjoy some peace and quiet. And drink coffee in their garden.

She'll find a new job! Teachers are needed everywhere. A teacher in the countryside has a good life; the villagers will bring her eggs and potatoes. There's plenty of food in the countryside. People in villages never starve to death; a village can feed itself. It's been a long time since Halinka last woke up her husband so cheerfully, and she even draws a faint little heart in the milk foam on his coffee.

She once saw a beautiful, perfectly formed heart in a café—so unlike her clumsy, misshapen one. But it's the thought that counts, not the shape, she thinks, and she's struck by the desire to tell her husband about her plan, but she still needs to wake up the children. And in the countryside, it'll be possible to sleep an hour longer, then get on a bike and be at school in five minutes. And here? Up at six, then driving at breakneck speed through those congested streets, always in a hurry. Where are we rushing to?! she asks herself while stirring the porridge and calling the children. They finally come: sleepy and shivering, because it's a cold morning. And there's all that din of cars and furious honking in the street outside. But not for long; after they leave the city, there'll just be the singing of birds and lowing of cows. She could have a cow. When she was in primary school, her grandmother showed her how to milk a cow. It's something you never forget.

In fact, nothing your grandmother teaches you is ever forgotten: you never forget how to make the sign of the cross or ride a bike.

They sit down for breakfast. Halinka's husband's eyes are glued to his mobile phone; he's responding to email. He says he has to, because the world moves so quickly now as a result of these phones. 'If you don't write back immediately, the customer will go to the competition.' He often chides Halinka that she's clueless about business. She thinks he's probably just spending all his time on Facebook. But if he really were doing that, where would he get the money to buy her flowers on their anniversary? He stares at his phone, unenthusiastically eating his porridge. The kids are eating it unenthusiastically too, like every day. She's used to them complaining about porridge. But they'll appreciate it someday, Halinka thinks, because it's a long-term investment in their health. The essence of motherhood is listening to kids complaining, and she's used to it by now. She wanted to have children; it wasn't an accident. She knew what she wanted! She was more certain of it than anything else in her life. Once in a while, though, she has second thoughts about Stefek and the children. But the more often these thoughts appear, the more quickly she pushes them out of her mind.

They're the light of her life—the kids and Stefek. And she sometimes even contemplates whether, if she were to get a tattoo, the word 'light' should be on her right or left arm. Anyone can get a tattoo these days; a friend of hers even had the ichthus tattooed on her stomach, and she and her husband argued about it because he said it offended religious feelings. Her husband told her they'd never have sex again and stormed out of the house, but then he came back in the morning and entered her so hard that she screamed in pain. Fortunately, no child resulted from that.

But Halinka won't get a tattoo. She doesn't like irreversible things.

After breakfast everyone's in a rush, and Halinka doesn't get a chance to tell Stefek that soon everything's going to change. Stefek takes the children, dishevelled, and Halinka calls after them from the doorway, 'Zip up your jackets, it's cold out!'

And she can already imagine herself taking time off work, even though she's talked many times with Stefek, who believes in toughening up the kids, about how they need to get them used to the cold so they won't grow up to be softies. 'Okay, get them used to the cold,' says Halinka, 'but call in sick sometimes, too.' Of course, this is out of the question because his work is more important. The one who earns a higher salary can't lie around on sick leave—it wouldn't make sense! 'My boss fired one of my colleagues whose wife keeps him under her thumb, and now they're crying about how their unpaid mortgage payments are piling up and my colleague can't find a new job,' Stefek says on one occasion, but he immediately corrects himself and tells Halinka that he knows she's got good intentions, because nothing's more important than being healthy, but he just doesn't like those remarks she makes and how she walks around with her head in the clouds.

Halinka walks to the bus stop. It's one of the last times she'll take it. In her mind, she says goodbye to all the faces she sees every day. It's the beginning of the farewell, she thinks. We're leaving, we're ridding ourselves of this, we've matured, we're starting a new life! And she gets off the bus in front of the school feeling happier than ever before. She notices one of her colleagues getting off the bus too, but through the other door, and she also seems to be beaming with joy. She's done it; she's pregnant now, after she and her husband wanted a child for so long. Halinka wants to share her joy with her and the thoughts she had in the morning, but she decides not to because Stefek should be the first to hear them, not Basia. Besides, Halinka and Basia have almost nothing in common, not even school subjects, because Halinka teaches mathematics and Basia teaches art. Basia acts like a snob about it; she talks non-stop about painting, Dalí reproductions hang everywhere in her house, and recently she's even been infatuated with Beksiński. 'But to have a husband like Beksiński would be absolute hell,' she adds astutely. 'Spending all his money on records and cameras!' When Halinka reaches the school, she forgets about paintings and pregnancies. She focuses on her pupils. Soon she'll be leaving them too, but she'll give them her new address. They can visit her on weekends; they'll reminisce about the old days and get to know each other better. Perhaps some of them will even visit their golden-haired teacher many years later, with their families. They'll tell their friends that their old primary school teacher chose a more peaceful life in the countryside. Not everyone has the courage to take that kind of step! Stefek will surely agree to having visitors, because then he'll be sitting in his dream office, answering email and talking to clients. That's what his life revolves around now. He supports the whole family this way, so Halinka won't interfere with his work.

They have fewer things to talk about these days, although lately they've been reading the same books—first Halinka, then Stefek. But they often quarrel because Stefek prefers to read fantasy, rather than pointless real-life stories. And on top of that, he calls the author an arrogant prick and says that you only get to philosophise like that when you have a million in your bank account. Although he, personally, would only need about ten thousand to feel more stable in life.

The wind picks up as Halinka leaves the school. On the way home, she needs to buy cold cuts and cheese for sandwiches, and some vegetables for soup. She does more substantial shopping trips with Stefek on Saturdays; Stefek helps her then. They complement each other in this way. He could help out more, but since his salary is higher, it's okay if he helps less with household tasks—they agreed on this, somehow, without even speaking about it. But Halinka sometimes has a problem with this. It's Stefek's mother's fault. It's often like this with boys. Mothers do everything for their sons. They're afraid their sons won't do things properly and then the mothers will have twice as much work to do, cleaning up the mess. Or they just don't feel like sharing their knowledge. But Halinka isn't sure, because she only has daughters. And for some reason, they're simply more interested: they set the table before meals and put the plates in the dishwasher afterwards. Stefek isn't independent even in these matters, although when it comes to email, he's constantly responding—even on Saturdays and Sundays. One never knows when a client's going to write.

Halinka leaves the shop in a hurry. She forgot to get cheese; she'll buy some close to home. Then she'll tell Stefek about the plan—but only after the girls are in bed. Before then there won't be time for a conversation like that. For the occasion, she buys some beer for Stefek. So that he won't fall asleep in front of the TV, holding a newspaper or his phone. He'll drink the beer and unwind, and they'll talk. Halinka will find a song on the Internet and put it on as a segue into the conversation, to set the mood. And then they'll look at some property websites and check how much they'll get for their apartment and how much cottages outside the city cost nowadays. Maybe they'll even have enough left over to take a trip somewhere.

Stefek pops open the bottle and smacks his lips. Halinka laughs, and then they look deep into each other's eyes. Stefek freezes with the bottle in front of his mouth and listens to the song with Halinka. Suddenly, he slams the bottle down on the table and jumps up from the sofa, then agitatedly responds to three email messages that have just appeared in his inbox. He jumped up exactly at the lyrics 'all the bad things in life'—Stefek can't bear these words, he feels betrayed by them, deceived and hurt. And he's receiving more email than usual this evening.

15.
I'm No Philosopher

When one grows old, one should move to a new home. It's not good to die in a place where there was once life. All those clichéd images: a grandfather browsing through a family photo album, inquisitive grandchildren, the passing on of life experiences, precious advice from a man with one foot in the grave, a clash between freshness and an exceeded expiry date, a sweater that hasn't been washed for months—it's hard to find any truth in these scenes, but they sell well during the Christmas season.

I haven't opened a photo album since Basia's death. I never look at my computer at all. It's so easy to come across something by chance. A young father with a pram standing in front of an old apartment building. Loose corduroy trousers the colour of café au lait. Two photographs side by side, taken in an avenue lined with plane trees: 'Let's take a picture! First you, then me.' Our favourite park. My Friday afternoons with our daughter. Your leave of absence from work for health reasons. That world coded by pronouns no longer exists. 'Turning back towards life on the threshold of death interferes with the natural process of passing away,' my friend Władek used to say. While he was dying, he could still see a little bit, unfortunately, although his glaucoma was at an advanced stage. Almost a year before Władek passed away, we burned his photo albums.

I need to move to a new home. At least so I'll no longer have to listen to that woman on the other side of the wall. When she was a little girl, she used to come over to play. The doorbell would ring, you would open the door, and she would enter without saying a word and go straight to the girls' room. The girls felt anxious around her; she wouldn't let them play. She acted like she was better than them. Now she's fifty years old and hollers at her husband just like her mother used to holler at hers.

'What kind of home is this where I can't even drink a cup of coffee in peace?!' her mother used to shriek.

As for this woman—she says, 'Go chat with the old man next door, will you? You still haven't? How many times do I need to ask you, for God's sake?!'

Her husband counters, 'Don't use the Lord's name in vain.'

She retorts, 'Go to hell!'

I wait. I'm actually curious what he's supposed to discuss with me. I look out the window and see him go out, hunched over. He stops outside the building and lights a cigarette. His wife gives him a hard time about smoking, so he has to take care of it outside. He lazily comes up the stairs; he's not in a hurry. He checks something on his phone. I open the door and watch him from above as he ascends the stairs. It's clear he's not in the mood for a chat, and that something's bothering him. Maybe this conversation he hasn't had with me yet?

It's sad to eavesdrop through the wall like this. Kids running around. Dinner time. I gaze into the depths of the apartment. Oh, the little daughter is crawling around on the floor, pretending to be a puppy. She always wanted to have one. 'I've found a home,' she says, barking. She disappears. Now she has three dogs. She has to get dog-sitters when she goes on holiday, so that's a problem. It's expensive. I have a chair in my entrance hall because it's hard to listen while standing up. But far from the wall. I'm rather hard of hearing. The good Lord takes a bit more of my hearing away each day, but my eyesight is still as strong as it was many years ago.

Daytime is the worst. One eats any old thing for breakfast, then forces oneself to nibble a bit of something for dinner. On the same plates. With the same fork. At the same table. Though the food's no good. When my wife was still around, more attention was paid to it. 'It's better to eat light meals,' she used to say. Now I'll just grab a ready-made pork chop from the supermarket, and then have trouble getting up from the table. I need a nap. And then there's that moment when you lie down, and you wrap yourself up in a blanket because it's cold—and there's hope that maybe this will be the last time, the end. But you get up an hour later and don't even know how much time has passed or where you are. One gets so disoriented by all that sleep during the day. I lie there curled up, perfectly still, as if straining my ears in case my daughter comes to check on me: 'Are you up yet, Daddy?' She lies down next to me and spoons with me. She sits on top of my bent legs as if on a chair. Nobody's coming. I'm holed up in the extreme depths of this home that was once so full of life, pushed away from everything and tired again, because it's already dark outside the window, so now it's time for supper and then sleep. Quick steps on the stairs. Kids. I never used to run. Except as a child, on concrete stairs. The stairs in this apartment building survived the Germans, but they're beginning to crumble now. I always walked down the stairs quietly. But these kids have no respect at all—thumping around in a wild frenzy. Rushing for no reason. And that woman is hollering at her husband again! Complaining that he left the windows open and their apartment got cold. There's a draught from the window in my place too.

It's hard to live when there's unsettled business. What's he afraid of? That I'll be offended? We never talk to each other anyway. But he walks up and down those stairs in low spirits and you can tell his woman's been pushing him around. Anyone can wind up in that kind of place—everyone, sooner or later, ends up realising that their life is no longer happy. You wander from room to room, your apartment feels large now somehow, but what can you do about it—that's what you wanted in your youth. You mope around, and nothing seems interesting. You pick up a book, sit down in an armchair, and even switch on a reading lamp so as not to strain your eyes. But it's impossible to get into the book. Tiresome suspense. I know from my own experience, because when my younger daughter moved out, my wife and I fell into a state of malaise; we couldn't sleep. Empty nights, sad mornings. But things worked out in the end. We both found something to focus on. My wife got serious about gardening. An allotment garden, a gazebo, flowers. Some vegetables. I enjoyed it too. It's pleasant to sit under a tree, doing crossword puzzles. But I refused to rake any leaves.

Then there were classes at the University of the Third Age. What rapture! Once she invited some of her classmates over for breakfast. Like sisters! A closer bond with classmates than she'd ever experienced before. Four came, and she spent several minutes greeting each one. They embraced, kissed each other on the cheeks, and gazed deeply into each other's eyes. They gave each other their utmost attention. And I ran around the kitchen making coffee and tea, and slicing bread. All those specialist conversations. About modern art, for example. I've never even dipped my toes into art theory, so I didn't join in. It's embarrassing to blurt out something inappropriate or fail to appreciate a highly appreciated artist. That's why I never went to exhibitions, even though I'll readily admit I sometimes felt curious. That whole crowd was too sophisticated for me. All vegetarians. You couldn't joke about anything with them. I took the liberty once with an elegant lady who was wearing a beautiful fur collar because they were in fashion again. I remembered that my mum had a similar one. I said, 'Nice fox.' She asked if it was a joke. And I said I wasn't sure, maybe it was. And she told me that if I let my wife go out more often, maybe I would've heard that she's a Green Party activist, so of course it was fake fur. So then I spent the rest of the party sitting by myself.

I'll change spots now and sit on the sofa in the kitchen. I spread my arms wide, as if waiting for the children. They often hugged me; they needed that. Now this emptiness makes me feel uneasy. So I put my hands on my knees. And even when my daughters do come to visit, they're not keen on hugging any more. Maybe they'd like to, but they feel some kind of barrier. I don't know how I appear on the outside. There's no way to find out from a mirror, because people always make faces while looking at themselves. You can't stand in front of it and just look, undisturbed. An eyelid might rise. Your mouth might move. And a hair sticking out of an ear will start to bother you. Not that I have a bad relationship with my daughters. Just different expectations. Sometimes you have a clear idea of what you want and wait for it to materialise, for everything to work out on its own. But you don't reach out for it. Something holds you back. Needless ambition. And if you extract yourself from its clutches, it's in such a clumsy manner that any child would be scared of you. I think my granddaughters are afraid of me. I've never asked. They don't come near me. I don't insist. They look at me curiously, like I'm an exhibit in a museum. After you've gone downhill, nobody wants to touch you any more.

'Granddad, which room was Mummy afraid to sleep in when she would come to you at night?'

'Come with me, I'll show you,' says their mum, my daughter, who relieves me of the obligation to show them around and explain things to them.

This image of my daughter has always stayed with me. She would come to our bed at night, and I would lead her back. We walked through the entire apartment, hand in hand, and then I waited to see if she'd come back. She always did.

'I'm not afraid, right, Mummy? Tell Granddad,' the little one warbles.

'She's not afraid,' says my daughter, but I hear uncertainty in her voice.

'Such a brave girl,' I'm about to say, but the words get stuck in my throat, because what's that supposed to mean anyway.

It's an unpleasant image; it stays with me too long. I close my eyes and think about what I'll eat for breakfast tomorrow. Fortunately, someone knocks at my door. Probably the neighbour. I hoist myself up from the sofa. I bet he can hear the shuffling of an old man's slippers on the other side of the door. I stood in front of a neighbour's door like that myself a number of times. It took her forever to open it. Now I'm trudging through these segments of infinite time. I shuffle along with an ambling gait. My knees feel stiff. And he has finally come to me with his question. Soon the matter will have been taken care of. And maybe everything will be over then. Because if you have nothing left to wait for, you soon begin to fade away. The tension abates. 'I'm not much of a philosopher,' I mumble to myself when these thoughts pass through my head. I open the door.

It's a kid.

'Have you got anything to eat?'

I look at the boy. He's blond and is wearing a chequered shirt buttoned up to his neck. His hands are clasped together and he's twiddling his thumbs round and round. He looks past me into my apartment, with his head tilted to the side. I turn round, following his gaze.

What does he see there? It's dark. After the war, a neighbour used to visit my grandmother. She would bring some coal she found by the train tracks. Just a few nuggets. And she'd say, 'These are worth two eggs.'

'To eat?' I ask. Perhaps I misheard him.

He nods.

I have nothing to eat. I've eaten everything. I try to remember if I have any extra food tucked away somewhere, or some sweets. But I don't.

I knock on my neighbours' door.

'No!' The boy runs to the stairwell. He sits on a step and puts his head down on his knees.

The neighbour opens the door.

'The boy's hungry,' I say, pointing to the child. 'I don't have anything to give him... Do you?'

'Adrian!' the man hollers at the boy, who, it turns out, is his son. 'I'm sorry, I'm really sorry. He's being punished. He won't get dinner until he cleans up his room.'

'I cleaned it!' I hear as I close my door. 'I really did!'

'Not very well,' my neighbour answers.

I sit down in my chair. Silence on the other side of the wall. I gaze into the depths of my apartment. I feel as if I were perched on the stern of a ship moored in a port. Somewhere at the end of that darkness, far down the hallway, the prow emerges. And on it, a light appears to be moving up and down. I go to check what it is. Maybe someone's playing with a torch? When I was a kid, my friends and I sometimes shone lights at the neighbours' windows. It's been a long time since I last went into that room at the back of the apartment, though the door is always wide open. It's dark, so it was probably just kids. I look out the window. No one in the yard, either. Was I imagining things? I go back to the hallway and sit in my chair. I can hear a conversation through the wall.

'If you don't go and talk to that old man today, I don't know what to do! What else can I say to convince you to go?'

I look at the prow. I see a light. I go there. It's dark. I return to my chair.

'I've been asking you for a month… Or two, even. I remember talking about it when we went to the graveyard with Renia, and that was in November.'

'October, actually, because we spent All Souls' Day here.'

'Whatever! Two months.'

The light appears. I wait.

'Please go…'

'All right, I'll go.'

'Now?'

'Now.'

'You're a dear.'

I look at the prow. There's the light again. It's moving up and down. It glides up slowly, but descends very fast. The neighbours' door opens. The sound of knocking. Will it be the same tomorrow? And the day after tomorrow? I'm patient now, though I'm no philosopher.

16.
The Crow

Walk down the middle of the aisle. Slowly. A guy passes you. The future father of your children? Don't look too closely, keep your eyes fixed straight ahead. Your gaze takes in everything and nothing simultaneously. You're unavailable. Inaccessible.

Flyers: give them to people, but nothing else. The rest is aura. Radiate it. Don't establish relationships, don't create tension. Don't be from here. Be from nowhere.

This is our manifesto. My friend wrote it. She's in her second year of a business psychology degree. She works part-time as a promotional hostess. She'll start her own business eventually, but for now she puts all her energy into her job. I comply with the manifesto. I'm holding some flyers: 'Smart fridges. They'll take care of your shopping. One hundred cans of Coca-Cola included with each purchase.' They say hackers break into the fridge network and do some shopping for you. You're a vegetarian? You'll get five kilos of pork delivered to your door. Quit drinking a year ago? Tastefully packaged cognac will be waiting for you on a Friday evening. And you're going to have to pay for it, you fool!

At the age of twelve, I'm one hundred and sixty-five centimetres tall. I'm the tallest in my class. My aunt says I'm destined for a modelling career and covers of high-end magazines. My mum advises me not to set my expectations too high, and to always accept my body. Because it's mine. So I stand naked in front of the mirror and look for something ugly. I can't find anything. There's a photo of Robert Pattinson taped to the mirror. He's been watching me with an admiring gaze for a long time. He has seen too much. Time to go, buddy! I pull the photo down. My sister appears in the mirror. She agrees that I look amazing.

'You want Rob?'

'Sure,' she says half-heartedly. Younger sisters usually like getting stuff from older sisters. But mine doesn't. She's not interested in fashion at all. She prefers dinosaurs. Sometimes I envy her.

My friends are shorter than me and don't have a body like mine. I try to cheer them up—soon they'll bloom like roses. But only some will become models. The rest will be beautiful only in their own minds—which doesn't mean they'll be less happy than the others. I don't want my friends to think I put on airs because of my appearance. That's why I wear thick sweaters and loose trousers. The colours are neutral—mostly black and grey. Sometimes when I walk past slim, attractive girls I regret hiding my body and sneaking around like a little grey mouse. And I try to cheer up Basia, who's only one hundred and forty centimetres tall. I'm sure she'll grow. But Basia doubts it—her parents are short. At home I ask my dad how tall he is. One hundred and seventy. Mum—one hundred and sixty-six. There's no rhyme or reason to it. I write a text message to Basia: 'Don't worry Mum one cm taller Dad five.' Basia texts back:

'My parents are 141 cm tall!' I imagine them lying together in their tiny bed. I remember a photo I saw at a flea market—old people dressed in children's clothes. With little caps on their heads. And an inscription beneath them: 'God bless the young couple.'

My sister uses the photo of Pattinson as a bookmark.

'Do you like him?'

'Yeah.'

'When I was your age, I had a crush on him. That photo's been hanging on my mirror too long.'

'And now?'

'Now it's your turn.'

My sister takes the photo and gazes at the actor. She squints. She touches his face.

At the age of seventeen, I'm one hundred and seventy--five centimetres tall. Still the tallest in my class. For three hundred złoty, I'm added to a face bank. I don't have any commissions for a long time… But finally, one comes in: a photo session with gardening equipment, for a calendar. With a weed whacker, a lawnmower and a branch shredder, wearing protective goggles. Each month in a different bathing suit. My parents don't like these photos. My dad condemns the photos mercilessly.

'You've changed so much since the time when I used to carry you in my arms,' he says.

I walk through town with my dad. I put my arm round him. He keeps his hands in his pockets.

'In this shop,' he says, pointing at a grocer's, 'I used to buy rolls of film for my camera. Someday I'll develop them all.'

My sister and I will get the albums.

'What are the photos of?' I ask. 'Not us, right?'

'This and that. I took them when I was young. They'll be mementoes.'

Sure. I like my dad's photos. He only takes them in black and white. They seem a little sad to me. My dad says the lack of colour is more artistic and conceals technical shortcomings. Besides, with a black-and-white photo, you just have to put it in a frame and everybody will think it's an amazing work of art. When we're walking together like this, I imagine that many guys think, 'What a young chick he's got!' I ask him if that's how it feels when I'm with him. He tells me it doesn't, and adds, 'Don't use the word "chick".' I don't agree. Sometimes he makes a big fuss about nothing.

Everyone at school likes me. Except Basia. She's grown a bit taller lately. She's one hundred and fifty centimetres tall. She's got pimples. And what's worse is that she smears acne cream all over them. I can't look at her face.

'We didn't have this tradition in my family,' my dad laughs, waving his fork in the air after having impaled fusilli with it for the past minute. 'But anyway,' he says with his mouth full, 'girls with acne are sexy.'

And my mum adds that she has never squeezed her zits. I feel like I'm going to puke after hearing these confessions. I say thanks for dinner and head to the bathroom.

I look in the mirror. I had a pimple on my nose once. It appeared during the night. I didn't go to school. Oh, I'm so inconsistent! I firmly believe everyone should accept their bodies, but I couldn't do it that morning. It's easy to make declarations like this when they concern other people. I need to work on that. And I feel sorry for Basia. We've known each other since primary school, but we haven't spoken to each other in a long time. I've tried to talk with Basia many times during the breaks, but she always turns away. It's unpleasant to talk to someone who's a head taller than you.

My barely begun modelling career is drifting out of reach. They never call from the face bank. At dinner, I reminisce about the photo session I did for the calendar. Dad is proud of something: he has never written a poem. Later in the evening, I look at those photos. God, how awful I looked! Such a disaster!

At the age of twenty, I start working in promotional campaigns. One hundred and eighty centimetres. My dad doesn't like this job.

'Why don't they pick short girls?' he asks me combatively. 'Because they're less attractive?'

'Maybe because being short makes them less visible?' I say, trying to justify my profession.

'Why are you so tall, anyway? Who do you take after?' he asks.

'After her dad,' my mum says, laughing.

'He's not your dad!' my sister says.

'And she's not your mum,' I snap back nonsensically.

'In that case,' my dad interrupts this pathetic verbal scrimmage, 'we have to make a deal.' And he takes off his glasses, as he always does when he's about to say something important. 'You'll add some of your dirty money to the household budget.'

I run to my room and cry for a long time. My face swells up. My dad apologises. He was just joking, of course. He jokes a lot. One time, when I had a supermarket gig promoting cleaning products for glasses, my dad walked up to a girl I was working with. He was wearing ski goggles.

'Excuse me, can I use your cleaning service?'

The girl took his goggles and cleaned them, and I hid in shame between the bread and pasta.

There are promotional campaigns every weekend. They're getting more and more sophisticated. At the grand opening of a homeware shop, I lie in a bathtub with another girl.

'Two American ladies from TV—Alexis and Krystle from *Dynasty*—are taking a bath,' I begin, as if we were little girls playing with Barbie dolls. *Dynasty* is a show I've really got into lately. Dad downloaded it from the Internet and we're watching it episode by episode in the evenings. The other girls are getting into it too.

'You've got to see the scene when they get in a huge fight. They totally rip into each other! When will Blake finally get home from work?' I ask impatiently. 'How long do we have to wait?'

'Blake!' sighs the girl I'm working with. 'Blake, come home! Dinner's getting cold.'

'Our man.' I close my eyes and feel her foot on my belly.

It's great at first. But I guess it could be even better. There's no champagne in our glasses. Just some nasty lemonade. At one point a little boy comes up to us and puts his hand in the water. The girl I'm working with grabs his hand and growls at him like a monster. He pulls away and starts crying. His mother runs up to him, then looks at me and the other girl as we lie in the water, holding our champagne glasses.

'How rude! I'm going to call your boss!' she hisses at us while walking away, pulling her son behind her.

Last weekend: what a nightmare! Walking around all day in red dressing gowns at the construction materials fair. Terrycloth. I'm sweating like in a sauna. Customers look at us with interest, but they don't take any flyers. Married men, however, come over to talk with us when their wives aren't looking: about Jacuzzi tubs, bubbles, types of soap, anything, just so they can lurk around the girls. One stays so long his wife comes and pulls him away by the elbow. I pass them a few more times. They're both sulking. I imagine what it's like when she holds him by the elbow, never letting go, sometimes squeezing where it hurts the most. To make him remember!

The boss gives us a lift home. We don't have time to change first, so we head to his car in our bathrobes.

'Is that you?' I hear a voice.

I turn around. Basia appears in front of me. She's as tall as me now. She looks beautiful. There's nothing left of the Basia from long ago. I forget the hostess manifesto and give her a hug. She's a bit stiff. I don't know what to say—I'm so happy. That she's looking great, that she's grown taller... that the time has come, it seems, for her to finally flourish.

'Basia! What a surprise!'

'What are you doing here?' I see anger in her face.

'I'm working,' I answer. 'I've just finished.'

'In a bathrobe?'

'Unfortunately—bathtubs, bidets, bathrooms, Jacuzzis…' I sway my hips to try to lighten up this increasingly uncomfortable situation. 'Thankfully that's it for today. How are you doing?'

'You're walking around the trade fair in a bathrobe?' continues Basia. 'Aren't you ashamed?'

'But why?' I feel tears coming to my eyes.

'I've got to go. Grzesiek's waiting.' She gestures towards a man standing impatiently nearby.

'I'll find you on Facebook,' I say through my tears.

'I've changed my name!' She leaves, arm in arm with Grzesiek.

Ten or fifteen minutes later we're stopped at the side of a three-lane motorway. The recently leased Porsche has stalled. The boss is surprised. We have to push. We get out of the car in our bathrobes. Oh, how they honk at us. A guy in a delivery van films us with his mobile phone. I remember when Basia wouldn't talk to me. When she was a head shorter than me. I give the man the finger. Is Grzesiek good to Basia?

The next day, photos of us pushing the car are all over the Internet. The girl I was working with informs me. We wonder how to get that shit off the Web. The girl's parents don't know where their daughter works. This isn't why she's studying economics! Thankfully her parents don't use the Internet much. But those photos might end up on TV;

they broadcast all sorts of rubbish. When a friend of mine showed up at Manifa with the Virgin Mary under her arm, it ended up on the evening news.

I walk along with my head held high. I stare straight ahead. A guy passes me—my type. The future father of my children? I don't look too closely. My gaze takes in everything and nothing simultaneously. I'm unavailable. Inaccessible. I'm carrying a bunch of promotional folders from estate agencies: 'Cosy apartments in a green, leafy district, with special areas designated for neighbourhood barbecues.' One day, many years ago, I played with my sister right in this spot where they've just laid the foundations of the housing estate. It was summertime. At the edge of the sandy road we found a dead crow. It was lying on its side, large and warm. We crouched down to look at it. My sister's knees were dirty; one had a pebble stuck to it. We gave the crow a funeral. My sister cried. She lay down next to the little mound of soil and dry leaves. My sister was six years old, and I was ten.

'It probably died while it was flying,' my sister said.

Two years later, I would start growing faster than all the other girls.

17.
I'll Always Love You

Ever since All Saints' Day, Jarek's been moping around. He's had enough. His wife is afraid to ask him what's wrong—he often flares up at her and then refuses to speak for three days. It's hard to live like that. Jarek stands by the window. He smokes a cigarette. He flicks the butt and follows it with his gaze. The tiny flame disappears into the darkness.

Jarek clenches his teeth. The apartment's too small—just two cramped rooms and a dark kitchen. There's a bathroom, but it's tiny. And they've got three kids. He loves those snotty-nosed little brats, even though he shouts at them in the morning and sometimes shoos them away angrily. And that TV! It takes up too much space. It would be good to get a new one. Everyone would benefit from it—his wife watches series, the kids cartoons. The new TVs are healthier, too. A flat screen wouldn't be as brutal on their eyes when they stay up late at night. Because there's always something. Right when they're about to turn it off a film comes on, or a rerun of a football match. The highlights worth reliving.

Those new TVs aren't so expensive. He's been checking them out lately, without telling his wife. He browses through catalogues while he's at work. He knows a bit about them. You can pay in instalments, even up to fifty months. Jarek makes a mental calculation. One thousand five hundred divided by fifty… that's thirty. Not much. How about a more expensive one? He thinks back to his last visit to the shop. For two thousand, you can get fifty inches. He's already measured the space and checked that it'll fit. Even sixty would fit there. Rent three hundred, food five hundred, cable one hundred, and with the monthly instalment, that's nine hundred and forty. Earning sixteen hundred or so, there'll even be enough left over for other pleasures. He calculates. He'll light up another one, then he'll have two to help him get to sleep and one for the morning. He'll manage. If his wife got a job, she could earn a thousand or so a month. And there's the five hundred a month per kid from the government! They'd really get back on their feet!

He'll surprise them for Christmas. He'll just bring it home.

'I'll be home late today,' he tells his wife.

The day before Christmas Eve, there's heavy traffic in the city; everyone's doing their last-minute shopping. There's also the monthly kindergarten payment, Jarek remembers. Three hundred each. He suddenly grows hot; he forgot about that. Better get the smaller one, just thirty a month.

The shop smells of brand-new equipment. He quickly walks past the fifty-inch model, which he had his eye on earlier, and stops in front of the forty-two-inch one—for two thousand. The salesman is already standing there. They exchange some technical remarks and toss abbreviations around: DVB, HDMI, MP3. And Wi-Fi. It makes sense,

Jarek thinks. He goes to apply for a loan. The decision about the loan will be made within fifteen minutes.

The quarter of an hour passes slowly. Jarek stands in front of the shop, gazing with understanding at the people rushing around the shopping centre. They're like him. He empathises with them—such valiant people, searching for last-minute presents for their families. At one point he even offers to help a woman carry some heavy shopping bags, but she scurries away from him, startled. Pre-Christmas stress. Jarek doesn't feel offended because he's already imagining the joy from the huge, flat-screen TV. Maybe they'll watch *Home Alone 2* together. It's always on TV at Christmas time. New York would surely look beautiful on a screen like that. The quarter of an hour flies by pretty quickly.

The man at the customer service desk has bad news. A system malfunction. Jarek should come in after Christmas; it'll be even cheaper then. Things always get cheaper after Christmas. Jarek leaves without saying a word. The magic of Christmas has vanished. He finds the pre-Christmas crowd annoying again. He doesn't want to go home. To those cramped rooms, to that old TV. And the worn-out buttons on the remote control.

And then suddenly he hears a voice—resonant and joyful. A voice filled with the holiday spirit: 'Internet plus a phone equals a TV. And a small gift!'

Jarek just needs to descend one level. He takes the escalator down and finds the shop. The offer's still valid. The system works. They don't get malfunctions here. There's the TV, the phone, the Internet. And the small gift.

'No thanks!' Jarek says, waving his hand, but then he thinks of his wife. A soft toy. His wife loves soft toys. The formalities take an hour.

A talented salesman. Jarek would like to have a son like that. He can pick up the TV tomorrow.

'We'll set up your Internet connection after Christmas; we've got too many orders right now,' says Sławek in a sad tone of voice. Jarek notices the name on the tag pinned to the salesman's T-shirt.

He sympathises with Sławek. He'd like to hug him, comfort him. He would even invite him to spend Christmas with them. They could talk about DVB, HDMI, MP3. And Wi-Fi. Jarek feels completely different leaving this shop than he did leaving the other one. As if he were floating.

He won't be his usual self at home. He'll read a bedtime story to the kids. He'll chat with his wife. When she comes out of the bathroom smelling of soap, in the nightgown that Jarek knows only too well, he'll feel like cuddling. Surprised, his wife will give in to his caresses. They'll have a wonderful time and will stay awake together late into the night. Jarek will offer her some water. His wife will believe in him again, and in the world she had begun to forget. And she won't be bothered by their apartment with its two cramped rooms, or the children squeezed together within a few square metres. When they get up in the morning, they'll start decorating the Christmas tree. His wife will take out the presents she bought many months in advance and put them under the tree. Colouring books for the children, and deodorant for Jarek. And Jarek will take a shower and then, kissing his wife goodbye, will run off to work, where he'll wish everyone a merry Christmas, even those he doesn't like because until recently he thought they'd managed to create better lives for themselves than he had. And right at one o'clock in the afternoon—because on Christmas Eve the boss lets them go home earlier than usual—he'll run to the shop to pick up the TV set, which will already be waiting in a flat cardboard box, together with the contracts. And the cardboard box will have special handles, which will lead Jarek to think with appreciation about the packaging designers, and he'll take the cardboard box home on the number seven tram. He'll enter the apartment and will be met by a surprised look from his wife and the joyful shouts of his children, who, although they won't know what's inside, will try to guess. But Jarek will remain silent; he won't say a word. He'll just take the old piece of junk off the shelf and put it on the balcony, ignoring his wife's protests. Then he'll take the new plasma TV out of the box and place it on the table, but then he'll take it off again and ask the kids to wipe the dust off the table. Maybe he'll say it too loudly, because his wife will be sitting on the sofa with the kids cuddled up to her, intently watching what Daddy's doing. They'll wonder why he's behaving so mysteriously and not speaking, when he was so nice yesterday. And his wife will recall the affectionate glances and cuddling of the previous evening. And when he finally plugs in the TV and sits down, tired, in the armchair, they'll wait together for the first star to appear in the sky.

18.
Wrong Number

The week leading up to Christmas is my favourite time of year. Oh, how intense the atmosphere gets at school! Everyone's absorbed by holiday preparations, like putting gifts under the Christmas tree. And we're all so nice to each other. Even Kacper has stopped bullying Olek, but that might only be because the headmistress scolded him for writing a nasty nickname on Olek's jacket with a marker. The PE teacher is the only one who doesn't go easy on us; he made us jump over the vaulting horse on the very last day before the Christmas break. I got a mediocre grade for it. My dad says sport's important, but there's no need to judge someone's skill unless they're doing competitive sport. If he were a PE teacher, he'd give pupils full marks just for attendance, because it's really only about getting some exercise. Just like with dancing. Technique is unimportant and only causes unnecessary stress. My dad really likes to dance, but most people say he's bad at it. My mum says that too. She says he should just dance alone so he won't embarrass his partner by not leading her in rhythm with the music. Dad says that if it weren't for his determination and desire to experience simple happiness, he would never know the joy of dancing because negative people needlessly complicate everything. It's the same with skiing. We joke that Dad looks like he's sitting on a toilet when he skis.

'You don't know what pleasure is,' he says. 'Anyway, she who doesn't feel good when she puts her bum on a toilet seat, let her throw the first stone. Joy, not technique! Joy, not stress! Technique and stress are for graduates of technical universities.'

I already know that I'm not going to study at a place like that.

Dad's been talking about stress a lot lately, though he claims to be stress-free himself.

'I've never worried about what's beyond my control. I once took a work colleague aside and said, "Staszek, what are you so worried about? If you know I don't have a problem with it and I'm the one who'll end up in hot water if anything goes wrong, then what's the problem?" And you know what? Not only did he stop stressing out, but he gained confidence and now he's a leading member of the team.'

I don't tell my dad that Staszek is the father of a girl in my class, and she doesn't tell her dad that his work colleague is my father. In this way, we have at least one secret, because everything else in our lives is already exposed on Facebook.

And this is also why my dad decides we all need to get Christmas gifts for each other by the end of the summer. He does this so the shopping isn't left to the last minute, for one must start the holiday season in a relaxed frame of mind. This is the only way to really feel the Christmas spirit. My sister and I agree with him about that. Then there's no rushing from shop to shop. That's why I bought all my presents in June already, with money I got from my granny for Kids' Day. I keep them hidden under my bed. My sister said she'll be doing some crafts this year, and plans to make everyone a collage. I love collages. When I get one, I'll hang it in my room.

My dad comes home in a merry mood. Tomorrow's the first day of his Christmas break. I like my dad at this time of year. He's always kind and cheerful, but at Christmas time he becomes livelier, as if someone has connected him to a coffee drip. That's what my classmate says—the one I kissed in the school cloakroom in November. My sister and I join my dad; we sing 'Jingle Bells', we dance. Just like we used to when Mum was with us. We keep in touch, of course. We call each other once a week. Mum lives in Norway and works in a fish restaurant. She finally has time for herself. I'm sure she'll come back, but maybe not for a while. 'It takes a long time to recover from years of motherhood,' she said. And that worries me because we agreed she'd be away for a year, but this is the second Christmas without her. I overheard Dad talking to Mum. Dad was lying on his bed. He was talking on speakerphone. I don't like eavesdropping, so I quickly moved away from the door, but I heard Mum's voice: 'I miss you too.' And that helped me fall asleep. Because before that, I'd been feeling anxious. I even asked my sister to sleep in my bed with me, though I don't like sleeping with her because she always sprawls and takes up too much space.

We're just finishing breakfast when Stanisław, the postman, arrives. He's so funny! He's a small man with a moustache, carrying a huge sack. He's a whole head shorter than me. He and Dad like each other. Dad invites him into his office. He wants to show off his new camera, of course.

'Can I carry your sack?' my sister asks. She puts it on her shoulder and walks up and down the hallway. She calls out: 'Letters from America! Postcards from Africa!'

Stanisław has to leave. Dad shows him out.

Then we decorate the Christmas tree and listen to a Christmas album. It's a compilation Dad made a long time ago. The CD skips a bit.

'Next year I'll make a new compilation,' Dad says.

My sister and I wonder which songs will be on it. Dad thinks there aren't enough dance tunes on this one.

'Christmas is a joyful time, especially Christmas Day when you can finally have a glass of wine and celebrate the birth of the Lord,' he adds, walking round the table. My sister scolds him and says he shouldn't mock Catholics, even if he isn't one himself any more.

His act of apostasy almost didn't come to fruition because all his friends who were willing to serve as witnesses started to back out, one by one, so that eventually this role had to be filled by my friend's sister and her boyfriend, which the parish priest considered scandalous; he remarked that Dad would be reminded of it at the Final Judgement. Later, Dad invited them for dinner and it was very nice, although not even Dad could stand the music my friend's sister's boyfriend suggested, and they ended up arguing about it.

There's a happy atmosphere during our Christmas Eve dinner because Dad loves the taste of his own cooking.

He asks if we mind him eating with his fingers. We don't mind, and also put down our cutlery. The carp is delicious and the flesh falls very easily off the bones.

'But do carp really have bones?' Dad wonders. 'What's the difference between a fishbone and other kinds of bones? Are they the same?' He announces an informal contest, making sure we don't have our phones nearby.

My sister and I start thinking about it and consult with each other about various things, such as whether fishbones have marrow. As an example, my sister mentions goose bones, from which our mum loved to suck the marrow, making me feel sick to my stomach. Despite my disgust, she took everyone else's goose bones and sucked them too, because that was the tradition in her family.

'Fishbones don't have marrow, like animal bones do,' says my sister.

'That's true,' Dad says. 'What else?'

'Animal bones are hard, while fishbones are flexible,' says my sister.

'And osteoporosis, how does it affect the hardness of bones?' asks Dad.

We don't know what to say because we have no idea what osteoporosis is.

'Well, it makes them more fragile. And that leads to another question: can fish get osteoporosis? I don't know. I have no idea. How can I know whether osteoporosis affects fishbones, since I don't know if they're like other kinds of bones because we haven't resolved our contest yet, and all I do is free them from the meat—I give them back their original whiteness, return them to their original state. One could say the fishbones are "returning to their roots",' he concludes.

'If you said something like that to our history teacher, you'd get a failing grade,' my sister says. 'Roots are where you come from, your culture, your history, your homeland—at least, that's what he thinks.'

'What's that teacher's name?' Dad asks, leaning towards my sister.

'Mr Nowak.'

'A beautiful Polish surname. Can you tell Mr Nowak, your history teacher, that roots exist in mathematics as well?'

'I'll let him know,' my sister says, and then she plunges into the carp's bones, pulling off the meat and licking her lips. 'It's delicious this year. Did you make it with Great-Granny's recipe?'

'Don't change the subject, darling,' says Dad. 'The contest isn't over. And as for your great-granny, I have no idea. As a teenager, I didn't follow her culinary feats very closely because we had a small kitchen—and you know how it is in a small kitchen. Why didn't I watch her? Well, either I didn't want to interfere, because housewives don't like to be watched over their shoulders, and sometimes they might not feel like revealing their culinary secrets, like my granny, and your'—he says, pointing to us—'great-granny, who was famous not only for her wonderful carp, but also for her phenomenal Easter cake…' Dad stands to attention, puts his right hand over his heart and says, 'If ever there appears a better recipe for Easter cake, and the taste of it is equal to that of your great-granny Helena's, I'll give the author of that recipe a one-year scholarship. The problem is that my granny didn't have a recipe for her cake because she was guided by the "however much it takes" principle. "How much flour should I add, Granny?" I'd ask. And she'd answer, "However much it takes." Because she herself didn't know. She just had a feel for it; the good Lord had placed thousands of receptors on her skin to test stickiness and viscosity, because these are two different qualities, my dear daughters. And these divine receptors estimated when it was necessary to stop adding flour. There were five eggs and one cup of sugar, and some cocoa was added at the end—three tablespoons, which everyone knew. But the whole secret was hidden in the flour.'

We look anxiously at Dad. He has strayed far from the main topic—the contest. I'm about to bring the conversation back to its resolution when my sister says, 'But you said you either didn't want to look over her shoulder because no housewife blah, blah, blah, or…?'

'Great question.' Dad sits down and pours some *kompot* made from dried fruit. 'Very good. So, either I didn't want to look over her shoulder in that tiny kitchen because no housewife likes—'

'Dad!'

'Excuse me, let me finish my sentence so I can get to the point… And so, either I didn't want to look over her shoulder or I was scared…'

We don't say anything. Dad makes a face as if he has just recalled the greatest trauma of his life—for example, a paedophile teacher on a school trip to compete in a German-language competition. Double trauma. The classmate I kissed in the cloakroom in November told me a story like that.

My sister doesn't know what to say. Fortunately, Dad speaks first.

'I was afraid that when I learned the secrets of frying carp, I'd become a cook and spend my whole life slaving away over pots and pans, and that, believe me, was never my ambition.'

'Do you think it's embarrassing to be a chef?' I say with irritation.

'Not at all! I was just afraid I wouldn't be able to estimate the amount of produce that was needed: how many kilograms of potatoes to buy, how many carrots, and how much liver—sorry, it's Christmas Eve. I mean sturgeon.' Dad bursts out laughing. We laugh, too.

'But you've learned…' I remark after a while.

'Because I had to,' Dad says in a sad voice, glancing at a photo of Mum on a plastic surfboard in a lake somewhere in Brandenburg. 'Amazing!' he says, carrying the photo to the table. 'Look at the quality of this print… and it was taken with a phone.'

We eat carp in aspic. My sister starts to choke. Dad gives her a slice of bread and explains, 'Bread will push the fishbone down!'

'So are fishbones the same as other kinds of bones?' I ask, to conclude the contest.

'They're different, I think… Because there's no marrow. We can check on Wikipedia, to be sure. But after Christmas,' he adds, 'because Christmas is a time without Internet or mobile phones. Unless we want to try to call Mum.'

We try.

She doesn't answer.

We try again.

The number's busy.

We try a third time.

She doesn't answer.

'I'll tell you a story,' Dad says. We leave the table, sit down by the Christmas tree and look at the lights.

'People used to put candles on their Christmas trees,' Dad begins, 'and these candles caused many fires, and some families lost the roofs over their heads on Christmas Eve because a whole room can go up in flames in under a minute. There are many fire simulations on the Internet showing how quickly flames can take away everything one owns and loves. One's entire livelihood. Tragedies involving farmers who lost their swine in fires, free-range hens burning to death…'

'Dad!' my sister exclaims, agitated.

'I'm sorry, darling, but it's an inescapable fact. We have to remember these things because life isn't only about delicious Christmas dinners, but also tragedies. They're interconnected. In any case, when you see a burning Christmas tree, don't hesitate; you have to evacuate immediately. And you can evacuate yourself from many things—even from your life, temporarily, as Mum did. Or forever, like the man Stanisław, our postman, told me about recently. So this man, let's call him Roman, worked as a security guard at a construction site, did odd jobs, and played guitar in the evenings. Just for himself, because he had no friends. Was it because he didn't want any? It's hard to say. But one evening, he comes to the conclusion that his so-called stability has come to an end. He puts the keys to his apartment in his letterbox, along with a full month's rent because that's the notice period his rental contract requires before moving out, and leaves home. He takes a rucksack with him containing warm clothes, such as long johns, and his guitar. He goes to the train station. The street, the doorways that are so familiar to him, the pillars plastered with adverts, and the people—he feels as if he were seeing it all for the very last time. As soon as he passes them, they become part of the past. But he'll make a final decision at the station. As he approaches it, he once again calculates each "for" and "against", although he has known for a long time that not a single "against" exists. He has no children or other commitments. There's no woman in his life either, so no one will miss him. He feels like he's in a very comfortable situation. Not like the guy who lives in the room next to his, who bought a motorcycle on hire purchase. Roman doesn't want any commitments. At the station, he stands beneath the train schedule board. He doesn't know whether to go east or west. Or maybe north? But the Baltic Sea is to the north—a dead end. He comes to the only reasonable conclusion and chooses south. A train to Prague will be leaving a few minutes after midnight. Roman counts his money again. There's enough for a train ticket, food, and accommodation for the first few days. And then he'll see how things go. He could earn some money by playing his guitar. He has a few songs. Simple lyrics about a simple life. Then a man who looks homeless approaches him. But Roman detects no trace of the typical stench. The man is scruffy but sober. He asks Roman for spare change so he can buy some tea. Roman reaches into his pocket and gives him a few złoty. "And for something to eat," he says to cheer the man up. Then the man hands Roman a picture postcard. "That's all I can give you," he says. Roman remembers a song by one of his favourite bands and can already imagine his fingers sliding along the guitar's fretboard. He stretches out his hand but then immediately pulls it back, not knowing why. Because he wants nothing in return? Because he doesn't want to barter in this sublime moment when his life is beginning to follow a new, unknown direction? But the man is still holding the postcard and when Roman sees his hand start to tremble, he finally takes it from him. Out of pity, he thinks at the time. "Paris," he says, reading the inscription. He recognises the Arc de Triomphe. "Thank you," he says, but when he looks up the man is gone. He tucks the postcard in his notebook and goes to the ticket counter. He looks at the postcard again a few days later. Right after moving into a room in a small town a few dozen kilometres from Prague. He's lying on his bed, staring at the ceiling beams and the irregular cracks in the wood. He wonders how long the wooden beams will last and whether they really still support anything. Perhaps the main part of the roof's structure is hidden somewhere else? Invisible to him? Then Roman reaches for his notebook. On the unsent postcard from Paris there are heartfelt greetings, hugs, and kisses. The postcard is addressed to Janina Wilk, in the Slovakian village of Badín. He tucks the postcard back in the notebook. A new life. An arrival in a new place, several days in a rented room, and some "pay what you can" concerts in local pubs. He doesn't miss his old room, or the supposed stability he used to have. People like the songs he sings day after day. They toss coins into his hat. And because he's such a quiet, polite lodger, the hosts give him provisions for the road when he leaves. And that's how it is as he goes from town to town, from village to village, from room to room. On one occasion he even sleeps in a barn for two weeks. They need someone to help with the harvest. Then one day, Roman finds out he's close to the Slovakian border. This will be his new direction. He gets in a lorry. The driver, who's German, offers him coffee and cake baked by his wife. Roman praises the tasty plum cake and asks about Badín. The German doesn't know the town, but he gives Roman a map. He's driving all the way to Bratislava. Roman can't find the village on the map. He falls asleep. When he wakes up, they're parked in a long row of lorries in a car park next to a petrol station. Two Poles help him find Badín. Three days later, Roman is standing in front of a one-storey house. He fixes his hair and smooths his jacket, but doesn't know what else he can do to make himself look good. He rings the doorbell. A woman opens the door. "Janina Wilk?" asks Roman. "That's right..." the woman answers. "I have a postcard for you... from Paris," he says, and he feels tears filling his eyes because he's reminded of that evening and the man at the station. "Come in," says Janina Wilk, and she leads him into the house. Janina Wilk tells Roman that she's Ernest Wilk's wife. They came here in 1965, when it was still Czechoslovakia. They got married here, too. "Here, this is his story. It began five years after the wedding," Janina says, handing Roman a thick album. Roman looks at each page carefully. There are two postcards on each page. "The last one is from Berlin." Janina wipes away a tear. "It came two years ago, right before Christmas. When did you see Ernest?" "I've been travelling for the past two years. I met him a few days after New Year's Eve. That's when he gave me this postcard," says Roman, and he flips back to the first page of the album. "When I first met Ernest," Janina continues, "he was an unsuccessful musician. Right after we arrived in Czechoslovakia, he tried to start a band. Unfortunately, nobody wanted to play with such an amateur. He approached various musicians and showed them sheet music, because he was actually really good at musical notation. But he couldn't find anyone willing to play with him. Disillusioned, he decided he might find happiness abroad. The need to play music was very strong in him. I saw that the poor guy was wasting away, and that music was coming out of him all the time; even when he spoke, his words seemed to be following some kind of melody. Every sentence he uttered was like the fragment of a song. I had no arguments as to why he should stay. I wanted to be faithful to him, according to my wedding vows. So I didn't protest. And anyway, at the time I was thinking about his unhappiness and lack of fulfilment—that I would rather have him, God willing, at a distance but satisfied with life, than share my home with a ghost of a man. I was relieved when he left, and when I received the first postcard from him, I felt happy." They finish looking at the album. Roman asks Janina if she'd like to keep the postcard. Janina refuses to take it. So far, the postcards have been arranged in the album in a regular sequence, so the unsent Paris postcard would disrupt it. For her, the correspondence ended with the one from Berlin. She puts the album away and invites Roman to the room behind the kitchen, where there's a piano. She plays a piece for him that was composed by her husband. Roman has the impression that Janina's puffy fingers might get stuck between the keys at any moment and the music will die away forever. He leaves Janina's house. He feels that his journey has come to an end. He wants to return to Poland. But it isn't that simple. From city to city. From village to village. From pub to pub. In one village, he spends several days. Once, after a performance in an elegant restaurant, a man approaches him. He asks if a song Roman played at the end of his concert was his own composition. Roman replies that it was a piece played from memory, by Ernest Wilk.

"He was here yesterday," says the man. "He played the same tune… But on the trumpet. I have a good ear for music; I'm sure of it. He gave me this postcard." Roman takes the postcard, astonished. He takes out his postcard and shows it to the man. The same handwriting, the same greetings, and the same addressee. The next day, the two men go to see Janina Wilk. Nobody answers the door. While they're standing on her doorstep, not knowing what to do, a woman approaches them. "Janina Wilk died," she says. "The funeral will take place tomorrow at three o'clock. The cemetery is two villages beyond Badín." The next day, the two men join the funeral procession. And when they finally reach the grave covered with wreaths, Roman hears a voice. "She waited for you until the very end, Ernest." Roman turns round. A woman is standing in front of his companion. The man glances at him uncertainly, then hugs Janina's sister—his sister-in-law. Roman walks away. He waits for Ernest outside the cemetery gate. When he finally comes, the two men give each other a long, warm embrace. Their journeys are ending and beginning again.' Dad concludes the story, then reaches beneath the Christmas tree. 'And this is my gift to you, from the very heart of Slovakia—the city of Bratislava.' He hands us two identical packages.

They're CDs. There's a photo of a tall house on the cover. And the title: *Paris–Badín*. My sister puts hers in the CD player. Strong, rhythmic techno immediately obliterates the silence that followed Dad's story. We listen to it in astonishment. Dad switches off the music and reads the list of songs. They're all pieces for guitar and trumpet. My sister's still moving her shoulders rhythmically; she seems to like the music. Dad's clearly surprised.

'I'm sorry, this is a mistake.' He scratches his beard. 'It's supposed to be calm, soothing music, but instead we got music for "dark rooms",' he says in an agitated voice.

He puts the second CD in the player. The same. He rings the number on the album cover.

'*Volané číslo neexistuje,*' we hear through Dad's mobile, on speakerphone.

It's repeated three times. Dad dials the number, and again we hear: '*Volané číslo neexistuje.*' And again: '*Volané číslo neexistuje.*'

Dad shakes his head in disbelief. He looks at his watch, waves his hand, and rings the postman.

'The number you have dialled is not in service.'

19.
Little Goat

You watch her brushing her teeth, you're standing behind her, you observe in the mirror how intently she's brushing because she knows you're looking at her, she looks up, you see each other, you comb her hair and pull out the pins tangled up in it, then you lead her, smelling sweet, to her bedroom where your other daughter is already waiting. You read them a bedtime story, then you start looking for the little stuffed goat because your younger daughter can't fall asleep without it—the little goat that's missing one leg, the little goat that isn't a goat at all, but rather something between a horse and a cow. Then you switch on the light in the corridor and leave the girls' bedroom door ajar, and you make sure the front door is locked, then you tiptoe into the bedroom to check on the girls again, you cover them up with the blankets that have slipped off, and you smile at the sight of them sleeping peacefully and catch a whiff of their sweet, childlike fragrance when you bend down to check if they're breathing, but of course they're breathing, they're too old now to be at risk of cot death. Later, a muffled thump and a red glow outside your window rip you out of your sleep. You think it might be fireworks; you turn on to your other side and then you hear pounding on the door, a scream in the stairwell, and quick footsteps. You spring out of bed because you remember that fire many years ago. Your wife runs to the door, you stand there and calculate, just like back then, what to take with you, what to save from the fire, you think about the computer with all the photos on it, your mobile phone, and then finally you remember the kids, but your wife has already thought about them, so you run out into the stairwell carrying one daughter, your wife carrying the other. But there's no fire, so you stop, and your neighbour tells you that they're arresting people, they're shooting, the army is in the street, but you're barefoot and in your pyjamas, the elastic in your pyjama bottoms has worn out and they're falling down, you have to keep pulling them up. The girls are wearing such thin nightgowns and it's December already, this morning you scraped frost off your car for the first time this year, this morning you drove the girls to school, and now you have to run down the stairs, though there's no fire, but they're arresting people, and the army is in the street. What you've often thought about is actually happening. You've talked about it with your wife; she was the one who went on and on about these visions and infected you with them. You tried to explain to her that there's a web of interdependencies, that it wouldn't be worthwhile for anyone, that nobody wants it, but now you see a soldier with a gun rushing up the stairs. The soldier shoots and a bang resounds that you've never heard before in real life, a bang that sounds different now than in films, a bang that makes your daughter bury her face in your neck, just like she did on the first day of school when you led her to the classroom and said, 'Go and join your classmates,' and she walked in, but then she turned round and ran back to you, and you covered yourself with your hands so she wouldn't hit you in the gut, like that time she rammed her head into you and you almost passed out, and she hugs you and says, 'I'll be brave,' but now she doesn't say she's going to be brave because she doesn't understand what's happening, you don't understand either, all you know is that you have to get out of there. But then your daughter starts shouting above the racket on the stairs: 'Little Goat! My little goat's still in my bed!'

To which you reply that you have to get out of there.

'Little Goat!' she keeps screaming. 'I'll go back and get my little goat myself. I'm not running away without my little goat!'

So you go back inside to get the little goat and you see a soldier entering your apartment, he walks all the way down the front hall, and the room with the goat is right next to the front door, so you sneak in quietly, carrying your daughter, but you don't see the goat. Your daughter says it's under the pillow. And it's actually there; what an intelligent daughter you have, she remembers where she left her little goat. You pick it up, you run out of the room, but your daughter starts talking about the little goat's leg, how you can't leave the leg, because the leg is waiting to be sewn back on. Why didn't you sew it on? You were supposed to sew it! Yes, you were supposed to sew it back on, but you didn't, because you were doing calligraphy with your daughters, you remember what nice letters you created, the prettiest one was the capital A. Where's that leg?! It's nowhere to be found. The soldier leaves the apartment, he doesn't see you, he doesn't see you looking for the little goat's leg. You finally leave without it and run down the stairs.

'It's okay, Little Goat,' your daughter says. 'You're missing one leg, but at least you're safe.'

It's like every night when she cuddles up to her little goat in bed and listens to bedtime stories, but now there are no more of those books, no more falling asleep, no more hair being combed or teeth being brushed very carefully because it's expensive to go to the dentist, there's no bed with a warm blanket on it, straightened later in the night after it slips off, there are no more of these nights, no more checking the door to make sure it's locked—instead, there's a truck in front of the apartment building, and you see your wife and daughter in the truck in the middle of the night, sitting terrified in their nightgowns. You try to join them with your other daughter, but a soldier stops you.

'No room!' he shouts.

'But this is her child,' you say, pointing to your wife.

'No room!'

'Where are you going?'

'No room!'

'What's happening here?'

'No room!'

You manage to give your daughter to your wife; she reaches out to take her and the little goat. You push forward to join them.

'No room!'

The truck drives away; the soldiers stare blankly ahead. You see your wife, you see your daughters, you see the little goat that's missing a leg, you see them and you don't want to think that this is the last time, because you still believe that this is some kind of misunderstanding, or just a drill, and that all of this might be for everyone's benefit because the army needs to be trained in evacuating the population. Maybe it's because of the smog? You often explain to your kids that smog is bad, that it's poison. 'What do you mean, bad?' they ask. 'The *smok* that lives at Wawel Castle is good.' You explain that the *smok*—the dragon—that, according to legend, once lived under Wawel Castle in Kraków, is different, it's spelled with a 'k', while the bad one is spelled with a 'g'. 'Poor smog,' says one daughter, and falls asleep. You close the book, leave the door ajar, and switch on the light in the hallway. You're in bed, but then you get up to make sure the front door is locked, you cover the girls up again because their blankets have slipped off, and you go to sleep. You're woken up by a red glow and shots being fired outside the window, and then there's banging on the door. You jump out of bed; you remember the fire in the past, and wonder whether to take the computer with you. You open the door and something hits you, you fall down and hit your head on the cupboard. You were supposed to get rid of it yesterday, the day before yesterday, a week ago, because it's no longer useful, you need to buy a new one, a bigger one, your family's stuff no longer fits in this tiny cupboard. Your head hurts, and they run in and start looking around, they open the fridge, they take out the goat's cheese that you bought earlier today in Lidl—one of your daughters can't eat cheese made from cow's milk—you're supposed to make sandwiches with this cheese tomorrow morning, and with some tomato, making sure not to cut it too thick. A soldier grabs the cheese, tears open the package, takes a bite of it, then spits it out. Not everybody likes goat's cheese—you don't, for example—so you agree with the soldier. You'd like to offer him some other kind of cheese, such as cheddar or Swiss, but you've run out of these, and you forgot to buy more. Every time you go shopping you forget something, even when you use a list, and your daughter runs up to her goat's cheese and is about to grab it when the soldier pushes her away with his boot. You just stand there. Shots are being fired outside. Your wife looks at the soldier. Your daughter's lying on the floor, crying, you can't go over to her, you can't even move because the soldier's watching you. The younger daughter says she has to get her little goat because she left it behind, and so she goes to her room, but the soldier grabs her hand and pulls her back. And she says again that she has to go and get her little goat because she never leaves it behind except when she goes to school. Then the soldier starts shouting that there is no little goat and there'll be no little goat, because right now we have to stand there and wait, and then two more soldiers run into the apartment. One of them stops you and you have to stand there in your pyjamas, in those pyjama bottoms that are constantly falling down because the elastic is worn out, and you're afraid they're going to slip off and you'll be standing there half-naked in front of these soldiers, so you stick out your belly. This causes you to fart accidentally, and the soldiers laugh because they think you farted from fear. Then they take your wife and daughters and leave, and you stay there because you're being held back by the first soldier who entered the apartment. Your pyjama bottoms finally slip down to your ankles. The soldier looks at you, gathers the phlegm in his throat and spits, then walks away. You don't have the strength to move, you sit down and listen to all the footsteps in the stairwell. You can hear your daughter crying, and you hear her scream that Daddy stayed with the little goat. You try to crawl into the room to get the little goat; let her at least go with the little goat, if she can't go with you. You start to black out. But then you open your eyes and see military boots, and then the entire soldier rummaging in the fridge. He opens a jar of pickles and drinks the juice. Your wife has asked you so many times not to drink pickle juice because then the pickles dry out, but you can't resist, so you drink it secretly when she's not looking, and you have to force yourself to eat pickles because you really only like the juice. Pickles are hard to digest, and your daughter, after eating them with scrambled eggs, vomits all night long and can't even listen to you while you read the bedtime story. She just keeps rolling over in her bed, saying that her tummy hurts. You sit next to her and continue reading, massaging her tummy, and she dozes off, moaning. You tiptoe out of the room; you don't turn on the light in the corridor since she's already asleep. You leave the door ajar so you'll be able to hear any sounds she makes. In the morning, if she's still in pain, you'll have to make a doctor's appointment. You lie down in bed, you don't read, you get up again to make sure the front door's locked, you cover the girls up again because their blankets have slipped off, you touch your daughter's tummy, then her forehead—it's burning hot. They say fever is a good sign because it means the body's fighting. It's all because of those pickles. You lie down in bed, you fall asleep, then you're woken up by a muffled bang outside the window and a red glow. You go to the front door but you can't hear anything from the stairwell. Your wife comes up behind you and stands there; you can feel her breath on your neck. Single shots ring out. Someone quietly knocks at your door; it's your neighbour. He comes in and asks if you've seen what's going on. You haven't. The army is in the street, armoured vehicles, tanks! A military operation is underway; everyone should stay home and lock their doors. He asks us if we have any bread, because he forgot to buy some. You don't have any bread. You should have bought some that morning, but you forgot. You don't like going shopping in the morning, leaving the warmth of your home and going out into the cold, standing in line, and not having exact change to pay for the bread. At the bakery, they don't have any change to give first thing in the morning, right after opening. Someone is running up the stairs, you double-lock the door, you push a chair up to it, then a second one, and a third, then the cupboard you've been planning to throw away for the past week, because it's too small, you need to buy a bigger one. Your wife is crying, and your daughter is calling out from her room that her tummy doesn't hurt any more.

'Can I go to school tomorrow?' she asks when you sit down next to her on the bed.

The teacher is supposed to give back their tests, your daughter made two mistakes, but that's okay, right? Anyone can make a mistake. Yes, those are your words.

'Only a person who never does anything never makes mistakes,' says your older daughter, who has just woken up because of the light being switched on and the red glow outside the window. And the sound of gunshots in the street.

'Promise you'll sew the little goat's leg back on tomorrow,' your younger daughter pleads.

'Today,' her sister corrects her.

About the translator:

Scotia Gilroy is a writer and translator from Vancouver, Canada. She has been living in Kraków, Poland, for over a decade, where she works for many publishing houses as a translator of Polish literature. Her work has been published by *Asymptote*, *B O D Y Literary Journal*, *Widma*, *Reflex Fiction*, *Armstrong Literary*, *Panel Magazine*, Comma Press and Indiana University Press. She divides her time between Europe and the off-grid wilderness of Northern California.